WINGS
OF
FIRE

WINGS OF FIRE

ESCAPING PERIL

by
TUI T. SUTHERLAND

SCHOLASTIC INC.

Text copyright © 2016 by Tui T. Sutherland
Map and border design © 2016 by Mike Schley
Dragon illustrations © 2016 by Joy Ang

This book was originally published in hardcover by Scholastic Press in 2016.

ISBN 978-0-545-68545-0

10 9 8 7 6 5 4 3   20 21 22 23 24

Printed in China   145
This Edition First Printing, June 2019
Book design by Phil Falco

For Jack — may you be bold and kind
and starry-eyed, and may you always save
the world your own way.

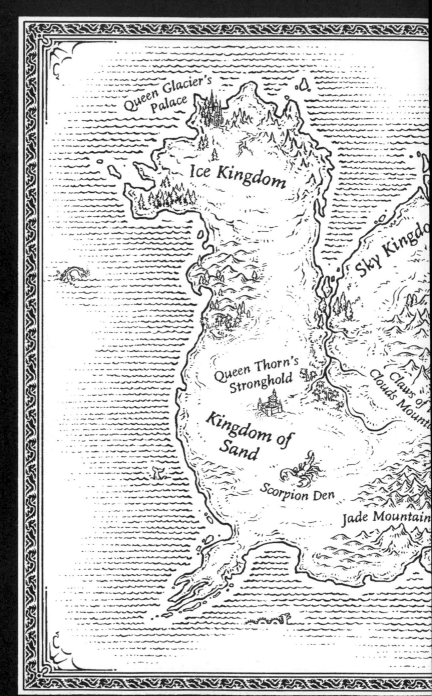

Ice Kingdom

Kingdom

A GUIDE TO THE
DRAGONS

Sand

Scorpion Den

Jade Mountain

OF PYRRHIA

UPDATED AND EDITED BY
STARFLIGHT OF THE NIGHTWINGS

WELCOME TO THE JADE MOUNTAIN ACADEMY!

At this school, you will be learning side by side with dragons from all the other tribes, so we wanted to give you some basic information that may be useful as you get to know one another.

You have been assigned to a winglet with six other dragons; the winglet groups are listed on the following page.

Thank you for being a part of this school. You are the hope of Pyrrhia's future. You are the dragons who can bring lasting peace to this world.

WE WISH YOU ALL THE POWER OF WINGS OF FIRE!

JADE WINGLET

IceWing: Winter
MudWing: Umber
NightWing: Moonwatcher
RainWing: Kinkajou
SandWing: Qibli
SeaWing: Turtle
SkyWing: Carnelian

GOLD WINGLET

IceWing: Icicle
MudWing: Sora
NightWing: Bigtail
RainWing: Tamarin
SandWing: Onyx
SeaWing: Pike
SkyWing: Flame

SILVER WINGLET

IceWing: Changbai
MudWing: Sepia
NightWing: Fearless
RainWing: Boto
SandWing: Ostrich
SeaWing: Anemone
SkyWing: Thrush

COPPER WINGLET

IceWing: Alba
MudWing: Marsh
NightWing: Mindreader
RainWing: Coconut
SandWing: Pronghorn
SeaWing: Snail
SkyWing: Peregrine

QUARTZ WINGLET

IceWing: Ermine
MudWing: Newt
NightWing: Mightyclaws
RainWing: Siamang
SandWing: Arid
SeaWing: Barracuda
SkyWing: Garnet

SANDWINGS

Description: pale gold or white scales the color of desert sand; poisonous barbed tail; forked black tongues

Abilities: can survive a long time without water, poison enemies with the tips of their tails like scorpions, bury themselves for camouflage in the desert sand, breathe fire

Queen: since the end of the War of SandWing Succession, Queen Thorn

Students at Jade Mountain: Arid, Onyx, Ostrich, Pronghorn, Qibli

MUDWINGS

Description: thick, armored brown scales, sometimes with amber and gold underscales; large, flat heads with nostrils on top of the snout

Abilities: can breathe fire (if warm enough), hold their breath for up to an hour, blend into large mud puddles; usually very strong

Queen: Queen Moorhen

Students at Jade Mountain: Marsh, Newt, Sepia, Sora, Umber

SKYWINGS

Description: red-gold or orange scales; enormous wings

Abilities: powerful fighters and fliers, can breathe fire

Queen: Queen Ruby (although some dragons still support Queen Scarlet, who may be alive and in hiding)

Students at Jade Mountain: Carnelian, Flame, Garnet, Peregrine, Thrush

SEAWINGS

Description: blue or green or aquamarine scales; webs between their claws; gills on their necks; glow-in-the-dark stripes on their tails/snouts/underbellies

Abilities: can breathe underwater, see in the dark, create huge waves with one splash of their powerful tails; excellent swimmers

Queen: Queen Coral

Students at Jade Mountain: Anemone, Barracuda, Pike, Snail, Turtle

ICEWINGS

Description: silvery scales like the moon or pale blue like ice; ridged claws to grip the ice; forked blue tongues; tails narrow to a whip-thin end

Abilities: can withstand subzero temperatures and bright light, exhale a deadly frostbreath

Queen: Queen Glacier

Students at Jade Mountain: Alba, Changbai, Ermine, Icicle, Winter

RAINWINGS

Description: scales constantly shift colors, usually bright like birds of paradise; prehensile tails

Abilities: can camouflage their scales to blend into their surroundings; shoot a deadly venom from their fangs

Queen: Queen Glory

Students at Jade Mountain: Boto, Coconut, Kinkajou, Siamang, Tamarin

NIGHTWINGS

Description: purplish-black scales and scattered silver scales on the underside of their wings, like a night sky full of stars; forked black tongues

Abilities: can breathe fire, disappear into dark shadows; once known for reading minds and foretelling the future, but no longer

Queen: Queen Glory (see recent scrolls on the NightWing Exodus and the RainWing Royal Challenge)

Students at Jade Mountain: Bigtail, Fearless, Mightyclaws, Mindreader, Moonwatcher

THE
JADE MOUNTAIN
PROPHECY

Beware the darkness of dragons,
Beware the stalker of dreams,
Beware the talons of power and fire,
Beware one who is not what she seems.

Something is coming to shake the earth,
Something is coming to scorch the ground.
Jade Mountain will fall beneath thunder and ice
Unless the lost city of night can be found.

PROLOGUE

Seven Years Ago . . .

No dragon was safe in the Sky Palace, but the ones in the most danger by far were the daughters of Queen Scarlet.

Or was it now daughter, singular?

Ruby hadn't seen her sister, Tourmaline, in three days.

Not since the night they went flying together and, high in the starlit sky, glowing in the light of two of the moons, Tourmaline had whispered that she was almost ready.

"Don't be an idiot. You're only ten, and furthermore, you'll never be ready," Ruby had whispered back. "She killed her mother plus all three of her sisters and eleven of ours. There's no way to defeat her."

"She can't be queen forever," Tourmaline said.

"She *has* been queen forever," Ruby argued.

"Twenty-four years is a long time but not *that* long," said Tourmaline. "Queen Oasis was queen longer than that, and look what happened to her."

"Are you planning to throw a scavenger at Mother?"

Ruby asked. "Because I'm sure she'd appreciate a snack before she kills you."

"It's always going to be like this," Tourmaline hissed. She flicked clouds away with her dark orange wings. "Until one of us challenges her and wins. You and I are the only ones left now — the only hope the SkyWings have of a decent queen. Ruby, if I defeat her and become queen, we can get out of this war."

Ruby wasn't so sure about that. She'd met Burn, and she suspected the SandWing wouldn't let her allies go that easily. But it didn't matter — there was no way Tourmaline could win a battle with their mother.

"The prophecy will take care of the war," she argued. "The brightest night is in four days . . ."

"Right." Tourmaline rolled her eyes. "I'll just wait for a bunch of eggs that haven't even hatched yet to save us. Ruby, I don't want to wait for things to happen to me. I want to *make* them happen."

"I don't want to watch you die," Ruby growled.

Her sister hovered in front of her for a moment. Stars glittered in her eyes, searching Ruby's.

She's wondering if I want the throne for myself, Ruby thought. *She thinks I'm trying to talk her out of it because* I'm *planning something. Like I'm that stupid.*

"Well, don't worry, I won't do it yet," Tourmaline promised. "Another few months of training, maybe. I'm feeling really strong, though. I beat Vermilion in a fight the other day. Want to hear about it?"

Ruby had listened to the entire long play-by-play of each move Tourmaline had made. They'd spent an hour soaring around the peaks in the moonlight. And not once had Tourmaline said anything about leaving the palace.

But then she was gone. And the most unsettling thing was, no one had even mentioned her absence. Her squadron was still here, training and hunting as though nothing odd had happened. There were no patrols out looking for her, no search parties scouring the woods, no missives flying out to other queens to ask if they'd seen (or abducted) the older SkyWing princess.

Just a quiet vanishing into thin air.

Ruby stood in the room she shared with her sister, studying the piles of blankets, the scrolls carelessly tossed aside, the gold-tasseled yellow curtains flapping at the window.

There were no splatters of blood. No sign of a struggle. No note saying, "Oh, I've popped off to one of the outposts for a few days, see you soon."

Did Tourmaline change her mind and run away? Could she have gone to find the Talons of Peace?

But Ruby knew that wasn't what had happened. Her big sister wasn't the kind to ever run away. More significantly, Queen Scarlet would never let the peace movement get their claws on her daughter. She'd find them and destroy them all first.

Heavy talons were slowly squeezing Ruby's insides, digging their claws in harder every minute that Tourmaline was gone.

If she found out that Tourmaline was planning to challenge her . . .

What did Mother do?

"Princess Ruby."

She jumped and whirled around. The guard in the doorway cleared his throat.

"The queen has requested your presence in the throne room," he said. "Immediately."

"Requested?" Ruby echoed.

The expression on his face said quite clearly that he didn't approve of the question.

Never let them see that you're terrified, that's what Tourmaline said. *Act like a queen so that one day they'll be cheering for you to slit Mother's throat.*

But now Tourmaline was gone. And perhaps acting like a queen was exactly what had gotten her killed.

"Thank you," Ruby said, inclining her head at the guard as she went past him. Her heartbeat drummed through her shoulders and out to her wing tips. The tunnel felt too small, as though she were the size of a thousand-year-old dragon instead of just a five-year-old dragonet.

Whatever happened to Tourmaline . . . am I next?

Dragons huddled by the throne room entrance, whispering; they all straightened their heads and wings as she approached. Curiosity gleamed in their eyes. They must have known Tourmaline was missing, even if no one would talk about it. They must have been wondering, like Ruby was, whether Queen Scarlet had decided to dispose of all her potential, threatening heirs.

But I'm *not threatening. I'm not!*

Ruby ducked her long neck as she entered the room, blinking in the blaze of sunlight that reflected off all the gold inlaid in the walls. It felt like walking into a funeral pyre; oppressive heat and the smell of dragon fire, radiating off the crowd of courtiers, closed in around her scales.

Queen Scarlet wouldn't kill her daughter in front of all these dragons, would she?

"Ah, Ruby." The queen's voice lilted over all the others, and the room fell silent. "At last. Court, many of you don't know my daughter Ruby because she's been away in training, and even when she is here, she mostly sits in her cave like a sleepy bat. If you ever *have* seen her, she's probably had her nose in a scroll. But despite the fact that she's nothing like me, she is still somehow my daughter."

There was a dutiful smattering of applause.

"Well, now everyone is here! Everyone important, I mean. I have such a thrilling announcement. Ruby, don't lurk by the wall like a jittery centipede. Come stand by your brothers. I want you *especially* to see this."

The crowd parted to let Ruby through, their avid orange and amber eyes peeling off her scales as she slid by. There was just enough space for her to fit between Vermilion and Hawk, both of them towering over her. Her other two brothers were on Hawk's other side. All of Scarlet's children were here except Tourmaline.

Vermilion snorted and edged a step away from her, but Hawk gave her a friendlyish nudge of acknowledgment. Ruby always got the feeling that Hawk was cheerfully being nice to her because he knew she'd be dead soon. He'd seen the rest of his sisters die under Scarlet's claws. Ruby suspected his good humor came from the security of knowing *he* could never have the throne, so he wasn't worth killing.

Their mother glowed like a poisonous orange from the top of her throne, peering down at the dragons that packed the room. The sharp sparkle of diamonds above her eyes and along her wings seized the light.

Ruby's breath caught in her throat at the sight of the hulking dragon at the queen's side: Burn, their SandWing ally, her face twisted in disgust and boredom. Everyone had been instructed to call her "Queen Burn" to her face, but Ruby found it hard to think of her that way. For one thing, she hadn't won the war yet . . . and for another, there was only one queen in Ruby's world, closing her deadly talons around everything in it.

On the other side of Queen Scarlet was a tall, oddly piled arrangement of black rocks that seemed to be smoking.

"Finally," Scarlet said, rolling her eyes as though including the rest of the court in her impatience with Ruby. A chuckle eddied around the crowd.

"Get on with it," Burn snapped.

Queen Scarlet flicked her tail and stretched her wings with deliberate languor. Ruby had time to wonder if the thrilling announcement had anything to do with Tourmaline ("I have thrillingly murdered one daughter! Why stop there? Who needs daughters anyway, right?").

"You may all have heard of a certain . . . prophecy," Queen Scarlet said instead. "Mumbling about special dragonets who will hatch on the brightest night and stop the war. And you may all have noticed that the brightest night is tonight. Isn't that terribly exciting? Tiny little heroes crawling out of their eggs any minute now! That is . . . unless something simply *dreadful* happens, of course."

She cast a sidelong glance at Burn, smiling maliciously. "What you all don't know is that someone tried to steal a SkyWing egg last night."

A gasp ran around the room.

"I *know*," said Queen Scarlet. "A nasty IceWing thief got all the way in here and actually escaped with an egg — the largest one in the hatchery, as it happens."

The air crackled as if it might burst into flames at any moment. Ruby tried to imagine life as a SkyWing raised outside the Sky Kingdom. The thief couldn't have been planning to take it to the Ice Kingdom. A SkyWing would never survive there.

So was he one of the Talons of Peace? Were they assembling the dragonets of the prophecy?

Was the dragonet in that stolen egg going to save them all?

"Oh, don't worry," her mother said. "Queen Burn chased him down, killed him, and destroyed the egg. We don't particularly *like* tiny little heroes, after all. Especially ones who might try to tell us what to do. So!" She clapped her front talons together suddenly, snapping the tension in the room like a bowstring. "Just to be perfectly safe, Queen Burn and I had a marvelous idea. We're going to make sure there *are* no SkyWings hatching on the brightest night. Not even one. Not even close. Bring them in!" she called.

Ruby watched in confusion as seven guards filed in, each of them carrying an egg. Red and orange shapes moved under the thin surface of the eggshells, and she could see cracks already spreading across three of them.

Queen Scarlet narrowed her eyes. "There should be eight," she hissed.

"We'll find it, Your Majesty," said the tallest guard. "I promise. She won't get far. And it was a runty one anyhow."

A skittering noise came from the pile of rocks beside the queen, and one of the stones trembled for a moment, then came tumbling down and bounced across the floor, rolling to a stop at Ruby's talons.

"Fine," said Queen Scarlet, putting on her annoyed-but-it's-a-celebration-so-I'll-just-kill-someone-later face. "I have someone *just wonderful* I want to introduce to you all, and this seemed like a perfect way to do it. Oooo, the suspense!"

A puff of impatient smoke snorted out of Burn's nostrils. "Always a spectacle," she muttered. "Can't just kill something efficiently and be done already."

Queen Scarlet ignored her. She was busy removing rocks from the top of the pile, slowly taking off the roof of the makeshift structure. Another scrabbling noise came from inside the rocks.

There's something alive in there, Ruby thought, and then suddenly a little head popped over the edge of the rocks, only a heartbeat away from the queen's talons. Scarlet jerked back, and Ruby was shocked to see something that looked like a flash of fear in her eyes.

She craned her neck to see better. *What could possibly scare Mother? She's not afraid of anything.*

It looked like an ordinary dragonet — about a year or maybe a year and a half old, with unusually bright coppery orange scales.

But then the dragonet swiveled her head, and her eyes met Ruby's.

Her eyes.

They were *blue.*

The weirdest, creepiest blue Ruby had ever seen, far beyond the color of the sky. Like someone had bundled up the sky and immersed it in fire until it burned from the inside.

That's it, Ruby thought. This dragonet looked like she was burning from the inside. Smoke was even rising from her scales.

Over Ruby's head, Hawk and Vermilion exchanged looks.

"Did you know about this?" Hawk growled softly under the hubbub of voices whispering all around them. "I thought it was dead. It *should* be dead."

"Don't question the queen," Vermilion muttered back, keeping his eyes forward and his mouth tensely still.

"It's an abomination," Hawk hissed. "SkyWing law commands us to kill creatures like that at hatching."

Ruby had a dim memory now of something that had happened over a year ago — an egg hatching with twins inside, the mother trying to escape with both of them. The palace had been in an uproar for weeks. But Ruby got only tiny scraps of gossip, usually through Tourmaline if she was lucky.

She'd thought they were all dead . . . the twins and the mother.

Could this be the one with too much fire?

The strange dragonet squeaked and tried to scramble up to the top of the rock wall, her tiny wings flapping hopefully.

Scarlet seized a long metal scepter propped beside her throne and jabbed the center of it into the dragonet's chest.

"Down," she snarled.

The dragonet fell back with a yelp. As Scarlet withdrew the scepter, Ruby could see that the round tip of it had a blobby melted spot where it had touched the dragonet's scales. A worrying molten metal smell joined the heat in the room.

"Your Majesty," said a squat rust-colored dragon near the front of the crowd. He was one of the oldest dragons in the palace and had served as an advisor to Ruby's grandmother when she was queen. Whenever he saw Ruby, he invariably made an odd clicking sound with his teeth, commented on how peculiarly long her neck was, and told her that the secret of long life was eating a goat kidney every day. And yet she could never remember his name. She and Tourmaline called him Kidney Breath.

"Ahem," said Kidney Breath importantly, waiting for the murmurs to die down and for everyone to look at him. "Your Majesty, please assure us that this is not what it looks like."

Queen Scarlet gave him a glittering, all-teeth smile. "Does it look like I have the most fabulously dangerous new toy? Because that's exactly what *this* is." She flourished one of her wings in the dragonet's direction. "Behold, my new and future champion!"

The dragonet poked her head out again, regarding them all with those sinister blue eyes. She glanced up at Scarlet's wing overhead and reached for it, but the queen kept it well out of her grasp.

"Your Majesty is the wisest of all dragons," said Kidney Breath. "Your every thought is genius and all your decisions are perfect in every way. But . . . are you sure this is safe? Keeping that . . . that monster alive?"

"She's not just any monster," Scarlet said smugly. "She's *my* monster. And she's so very useful. Here, darling, show them what you can do." The queen plucked one of the eggs from a guard's talons and passed it casually to the dragonet.

At least . . . she made it look casual, but Ruby could see how carefully Scarlet avoided touching the dragonet's claws, and how quickly she snatched her talons back.

The dragonet looked down at the egg, which was almost a quarter of her own size. Her expression was curious and a little delighted, as if no one had ever given her a toy before.

And then small tremors began to run across the eggshell, and the translucent whiteness began to fade to gray, and the orange shape inside gave a shudder and then turned black, black as coals, black as dead, burnt husks of trees, before the whole egg went black and no one could see inside anymore.

A hush fell over the room.

Nobody spoke. *Nobody* could *speak,* Ruby thought. She felt as though she couldn't even breathe. Like perhaps it would be safer to never breathe again.

The egg crumbled into a pile of ash in the dragonet's talons.

The dragonet stared down at her claws with an unreadable expression. Was she surprised? Pleased with herself? Did she know that with one simple act — by merely holding an egg — she'd managed to terrify every dragon in the room?

She tilted her head slightly to peer up at the queen, and in that moment Ruby caught a glimpse of something familiar in those weird eyes.

The dragonet with too much fire was worried that Scarlet would be angry with her.

It was Burn who finally broke the silence. "Impressive," she growled. "Now deal with the rest of them, or let me smash them myself."

Scarlet reached over with the scepter and knocked down the wall of rocks in the dragonet's way. "Go touch the rest of the eggs, Peril," she ordered.

Peril, Ruby thought. *The monster has a name.*

Peril glanced at the eggs, then down at her talons, then back at Queen Scarlet. She looked very small next to the two queens.

"But —" she said, her voice swallowed by the hot air in the hushed room. "But I burnded it."

"You are my champion," said Queen Scarlet coldly. "You do as I tell you to."

Peril hesitated for a moment, looking around at the

wall of scales and wings and unfriendly, suspicious eyes around her. She stepped forward, and the guards holding the eggs all quickly placed them on the ground, stumbling out of her way.

One by one, Peril stopped at each egg and laid her claws on it until the dragonet inside was dead.

She could do that to anyone, Ruby realized. *She can probably kill a full-grown dragon just by touching him. She's the deadliest weapon Mother has ever found.*

A ripple of horror ricocheted through her scales.

Is that what happened to Tourmaline?

She couldn't unhook her gaze from the murderous dragonet.

Is my sister now a pile of ashes somewhere?

As Peril reached the last egg, Ruby finally tore her eyes free and lifted them toward the queens.

Scarlet was watching Ruby with a satisfied, sinister look. A look that said: "Who would dare challenge me now? You, my dreaming daughter? Go ahead and try. If you even think about it, now you know whose talons will find your throat in the middle of the night."

She was right. No one could stop Scarlet now.

Ruby would never be queen.

Peril would always be there, the threat lurking behind the throne, the smoking scales that lay in wait for any dragon who showed even a hint of ambition.

So I won't, Ruby thought. *I won't dream of the throne. I'll be obedient, loyal, agreeable, anything she wants me to be. Anything that keeps me alive and as far away from that monster as I can get.*

You win, Mother.

The dragonet lifted her claws from the last smoking egg and turned to Queen Scarlet with a hungry look in her eyes. Ruby recognized that look, too — the "do you love me now?" look.

"Excellent," said Queen Scarlet, flicking her tongue between her teeth. "A thrilling demonstration. Everything I was hoping for. As you say, Queen Burn, so much for that prophecy now, right? Peril, back to your place."

I hope you know how to control your new champion, Mother. Because she's not just a threat to me.

The crowd of dragons surged back, struggling to stay out of Peril's path, as the dragonet walked slowly back to the little cage of rocks.

This dragon could destroy the entire world.

Ice Kingdom

Sky Kingdom

Queen Thorn's
Stronghold

Claws of the
Clouds Mountains

Kingdom of
Sand

Scorpion Den

Jade Mountain

PART ONE

SCALES OF FIRE

CHAPTER 1

Deep in a cave in Jade Mountain, the most dangerous dragon in Pyrrhia was hiding.

Which she was not particularly pleased about.

"Just until Ruby's gone," Peril muttered, pacing. "That's what he said. *Hours* ago. He said he'd come get me as soon as it was safe. Ha! As if I should be afraid of her. I'm not afraid of anyone! Three moons, it's been *forever*. How long does it take to collect a body?"

And why should she have to hide anyway? That's what she wanted to know.

Yes, she was banished from the Sky Kingdom, but Queen Ruby couldn't banish her from Jade Mountain, too. Clay had said it himself: this wasn't the Sky Palace. He'd said, "You have every right to be here."

Was that true?

Did she actually have the right to be *anywhere*, after everything she'd done?

But all she wanted was to be with Clay. Near him, around him, breathing the same air and watching the same skies. That wasn't asking too much. And if it meant she wasn't hurting anyone anymore, wasn't that what everyone wanted?

Maybe not. Maybe Queen Ruby wanted Peril to be miserable and alone.

Well. Peril hissed a tendril of smoke and marched to the cave entrance, peering out. If *any dragon* tried to keep her away from Clay, she would *melt off their head.* Even if that dragon was the new SkyWing queen!

Unless Clay told me not to, I guess.

Peril went back to circling the small cave, flicking her wings at the claustrophobic stone walls.

There had been a moment, months ago, in the chaos of the SkyWing transition, when Peril thought things were going to be different. After she'd helped Clay and the others escape from Scarlet's arena, she'd flown back to the palace only to find Queen Scarlet and Queen Burn gone and the whole tribe in a state of panic. Who'd be in charge now? What had happened to their invincible queen?

The relief when Princess Ruby arrived and took over . . . Peril remembered it clearly, with a wince of pity for her idiotic hopeful former self. Along with everyone else she had thought, *A new queen! One who isn't terrifying! Everything's going to change!*

It was true: everything *had* changed. For the better, generally, for everyone but Peril.

There had been no thank-yous, no celebrations or medals. Idiotic hopeful former self had hoped for them. Idiotic hopeful former self was very stupid.

In fact, there hadn't been any acknowledgment at all that Peril had helped the dragonets of destiny defeat Queen Scarlet. *I mean, they did most of it, but I did help. Didn't anyone notice?*

Instead, Ruby's very first act as queen had been to banish Peril from the Sky Kingdom.

Peril could still hear her hissing, "I never want to see you again" . . . and she could still feel the strange, falling vertigo it had given her, as if her wings had been sliced off.

Until that moment, Ruby had always been — not friendly, exactly — but not hostile, either. Mostly she'd been quiet. She'd stayed out of Peril's way, nodding politely in the halls or leaving the room when Peril came to talk to Scarlet. She'd never seemed very queenly, to be frank. So where did this imperious, decisive dragon come from?

"But . . . why?" Peril had asked, trying to ignore the expressions on the guards that surrounded Ruby. Why did they look so *pleased*?

"Because you're a murderer," Ruby replied, as if that should have been perfectly self-evident.

But aren't we all murderers? Peril had thought. *Didn't we all do terrible things because Queen Scarlet told us to? Can you find me one dragon who defied her? Why am I the only one getting punished for obedience?*

Then she'd looked into Ruby's eyes and realized it was personal. Ruby actually hated her. Peril had never known that — and even now, she still wasn't sure why. Hadn't they both been loyal SkyWing subjects? Hadn't they both always followed Scarlet's orders? Couldn't Ruby, of all dragons, understand everything that Peril had done?

"Leave now," Ruby had said. "Or die. Whichever."

And how do you plan to make me? Peril had felt fiery rage swelling under her scales. *I could kill you right now, as easily as breathing. I could kill everyone in this cave just by spreading my wings.*

She nearly had. She'd really, really wanted to. The only thing that had stopped her was thinking of Clay.

He said he saw good in her. Which *probably* meant he didn't want her setting large groups of dragons on fire every time she got mad.

He thought she could be more than Queen Scarlet's pet killer, and so, for him, she would be.

Well . . . she would *try*.

It was *hard*, though. Dragons could be *awful*. Some of them really *deserved* to be set on fire.

And she didn't *like* being told to sit in a cave for hours, just because the sight of her might make Ruby angry. The SkyWing queen was on her way to Jade Mountain to collect the body of the student who'd died, Carnelian. So, yes, she probably wouldn't be in a very good mood to begin with. Peril could understand that it would be easier for Clay and his friends if she stayed out of the way, so that Ruby's visit would go as smoothly as possible.

But WHY WAS IT TAKING SO LONG?

Peril paced to the cave entrance again, peering out into the dimly lit tunnel.

Farther along the tunnel, deeper in the mountain, the faint sounds of splashing and laughter echoed from the underground lake. The SeaWing students had decided the lake was their exclusive clubhouse and were there all the time now. Peril was always careful to avoid them. She avoided all the students as much as she could.

Everyone here was afraid of her, but no one was *careful* of her the way they'd been in the Sky Kingdom. Only the SkyWings knew how to steer a wide path around her. The dragons in Scarlet's palace had been experts at avoiding Peril; wherever she'd gone, empty space opened up around her.

Here, *she* had to be the cautious one. *She* was responsible for staying out of *their* way. Even though they were terrified of her, the other students kept forgetting she was there.

But what if she bumped into one of them? What if her tail brushed someone's wing by accident?

How would Clay look at her then?

He said she deserved a second chance . . . but if she burned one of his students, she knew there wouldn't be a third.

Peril's claws twisted and clenched, thinking of all the dragonets Clay was protecting here. Did he love them more than her? He must — he should — why wouldn't he? They were innocent symbols of the bright future he always talked about. None of them had murdered — her mind shied away from the numbers — a whole lot of dragons.

But none of them had saved his life either! *And* his friends!

Didn't matter. They still hated her, those shining friends who stood between her and Clay like blue and green and gold flames, flaring suspiciously whenever she so much as looked at him.

Down on the sands of Burn's stronghold, after she'd saved him, under the eyes of all the tribes, Clay had said, "Maybe Peril is our wings of fire." And for one surreal moment she'd thought, *maybe I am — maybe this makes up for everything I've done. Maybe by saving Clay, I've saved the world.*

Maybe everyone will forgive me now. Maybe everyone will love me now.

But that wasn't what had happened.

After the end of the war, Peril had searched for Queen Scarlet for months, all across the continent. And everywhere she went, dragons fled screaming at the sight of her. Or they fainted. Or they threw spears and rocks at her, along with anything else sharp or pointy or heavy that they could get their talons on. Once she'd been walloped in the face by a dead crocodile, flung from the depths of the MudWing swamps.

It was strange to realize that things like that could hurt more on the inside of your scales than the outside.

It was strange to realize that a dragon who *couldn't* be hurt on the outside could have so many ragged holes on the inside.

There! Talons thumping on stone! The rough slither of a tail! Was it him?

Peril nearly leaped into the corridor — and came within a wing flicker of colliding with a dragon who definitely wasn't Clay.

The dark green SeaWing dragonet didn't scream or faint or stagger back in terror. He simply froze, slamming his eyes closed as though danger would obligingly disappear the moment he couldn't see it anymore.

"What are you *doing*?" Peril yelped, jumping away from him.

"Um," he said in a low, rumbly voice. "Walking? In the halls? Back to my cave?" He risked opening one eye to peer at her.

"Well, that was VERY STUPID of you!" she snapped.

He thought about that for a moment, then opened both eyes and regarded her peaceably. "Oh," he said. "Sorry."

What a peculiar dragon. He seemed to have no fire about him at all. That wasn't a SeaWing thing; Tsunami was a fireball that blazed up and down and sideways at everything that made her mad (which was most things). And her sister, the little SeaWing princess, at least from a distance seemed to be a shower of bright orange sparks on the inside.

This SeaWing, on the other talon, was a puddle. A fireless puddle, blobbing quietly into the rocks in front of her, not even trying to get away.

"You're Peril, aren't you?" he said. "Queen Scarlet's . . ." He trailed off, perhaps realizing there was no good way to end that sentence. *Champion? Weapon? Notorious death monster?*

"Yes," she hissed. "I'm Queen Scarlet's notorious death monster."

He made an odd hiccupping noise and ducked his head. "Ah, OK. I'll just . . . go, then."

What would Clay want her to do in this situation? *Maybe you'll make some friends here,* he'd said, in that oblivious magical way he had of thinking that any other dragons in the world might have open hearts like his.

"Who are you?" she asked. *Hmmm. That came out more menacing than it sounded in my head.* "I mean, who *are* you?" she tried, adding a Sunnyish cheerful lilt to her voice. *Now I sound manic.* "I'm not being creepy," she added hastily. "I'm not, like, putting you on a murder list or anything. I don't have a murder list! Not a to-be-murdered list, I mean. Wait, no — to be clear, I have no kind of murder list at all. Definitely out of the murdering business, me. Maybe I should stop saying the word murder."

"That would be great," the SeaWing said. "If you wouldn't mind."

"I just did what I was told," she said in a rush. She couldn't remember another dragon standing still long enough to hear her say that, not since Ruby had thrown her out of the Sky Palace. "I was doing what my queen told me to do. Isn't that what everyone does? I can't help what I'm like — and what she made me do. Can I?"

Maybe it was that he didn't look scared. He didn't look *thrilled* to be having this conversation, but he hadn't run screaming yet.

His green-eyed gaze traveled thoughtfully along her smoking scales, shifted for a moment to his own talons, and then dropped to the ground. "I guess," he said. "Turtle."

Peril puzzled over this for a moment. Was it some kind of SeaWing code? Was he calling her a turtle? Was that a good or a bad thing?

"Moose," she tried out, just to see what would happen.

He squinted at her. "Uh . . . I mean, my name is Turtle."

"Oh!" she said. "Right. Hello. Thank you for not screaming or fainting or throwing a crocodile at me."

"I thought about it," he said. "I mean, not the crocodile. Definitely not in the reptile-throwing business, me."

Now it was her turn to narrow her eyes at him. Was he making fun of her?

"Ha ha?" he tried. "Friendly joke? Are those allowed?"

"Why aren't you scared of me?" she asked.

"I *am*," he said. "I just . . . you're not the only dragon I know with dangerous powers."

"Really?" she said. What did that mean? Who was he talking about?

But before he could answer, a roar billowed down through the corridors, like a rolling smoke cloud.

Turtle flared his wings, his green eyes wide. "What was that?"

"Probably Queen Ruby," Peril said. Was Ruby yelling at Clay? Was Clay all right? Did he need her to come protect him? She glanced back at the row of fire globes leading uphill to the school. "Maybe they just told her that I'm here."

"Want to go find out?" Turtle asked.

Peril frowned at him. "So I can get roared at face-to-face? That *does* sound more fun."

"I don't mean go say *hi*," Turtle protested. "I mean, *I'm* going to eavesdrop to see what's happening, so do you want to come?"

Peril curled her wings in, severely tempted. "Oh, no, I shouldn't. Clay would be upset with me. He told me to wait here."

"He doesn't have to know," Turtle said with a shrug. "That's kind of the point of being stealthy. And if he doesn't catch you, then you're not doing anything wrong, are you?"

That sounded true. That sounded very true! Really, Clay just wanted her to stay out of Ruby's way. So if she didn't let Ruby see her that was basically the same thing, right? After all, he didn't *specifically* say "you must hide in a cave for hours like an obedient snail."

Stop for a moment. Think this through.

On the one talon, she was still pretty sure Clay wouldn't approve of this plan. On the other talon, it sounded a LOT more appealing than sitting in a cave waiting to be released. On the third talon, why was this strange SeaWing offering to hang out with her? Did he have an agenda? Was it because if they got caught, she was sure to get in a lot more trouble than he would?

Then again, on the fourth talon, shouldn't she say yes to the first friendly dragon she'd met at this school? Clay *did* want her to make friends. So in a way she *was* doing something he would approve of. Right?

Unless Clay secretly thought she was too dangerous for anyone to be friends with. He might think that. She kind of was. Her only friend before Clay had been killed by Queen Scarlet for telling Peril too much.

Well, then, maybe she needed more friends so that some of them could be expendable. If anything happened to Clay right now, it would be the END OF ALL THINGS. She would literally burn down the world. She couldn't even think about it, or else the tunnel would soon be full of rage smoke.

But if she had Clay *and* Turtle as friends, and then Turtle got himself killed by Queen Scarlet or accidentally set on fire, well, then she'd survive OK, because she'd still have Clay.

It occurred to her that this was a rather morbid train of thought to be having about a new friend.

"Yes," she said decisively, making him jump. "Let's go. You walk in front, so I don't whack you with my tail by accident. But don't move too slowly, or I might accidentally step on you." She ducked into the cave again to let him by safely.

Turtle had an "I am now sensing this was a terrible idea" expression on his face, but he took the lead without arguing and managed to walk fast enough that Peril wasn't annoyed.

The roar echoed from above again.

Together — more or less — Turtle and Peril headed straight for it.

CHAPTER 2

For the past week, Carnelian's body had been kept in a cave near the peak of Jade Mountain. According to SkyWing tradition, their dead were offered to the sky for seven days before being burned. An old dragon named Osprey — the only one in the Sky Palace who would speak with Peril voluntarily — had told Peril that this was to make sure their spirits could fly free and return as SkyWings, instead of coming back as any other kind of dragon.

That kind of talk always made Queen Scarlet roll her eyes, though. She let her tribe follow whatever rituals they cared about, but she was not much interested in what happened to dragons after they were dead.

Peril had visited the body twice, at night when everyone else was asleep. She didn't remember ever meeting the fierce red dragonet in the Sky Kingdom, but then, she didn't know most SkyWings by name. Queen Scarlet didn't like it when

Peril tried to talk to other dragons. To be honest, neither did the other dragons.

So Peril had seen the mourning cave by moonlight — the tall arched roof, the towering slender pillars of pale gray rock, all the windows and skylights that opened to the air. And she'd seen the burned dragon wrapped in white silk, as still and empty as any of the charred bodies Peril had left on Scarlet's arena sands.

But she hadn't seen the cave in the daytime before. She hadn't seen the sunlight pouring in, white and gold and backed with blue sky, or the wind rippling the silk so it looked like Carnelian was breathing.

Now it really looked like a place where a spirit could be set free . . . a place where a new SkyWing might rise again.

Unless it was scared off by the angry dragons gathered around the body anyhow. On the plus side, at least all the shouting meant no one could hear Turtle and Peril sneaking up the passage toward them.

Turtle crouched behind a boulder near the cave entrance. Peril peeked in, long enough to see at least a dozen SkyWings crowding the chamber, and decided to stay farther back, keeping a few curves of the wall and several columns between her and the queen who hated her.

"I smell lies all over this story," snarled a SkyWing — not Ruby, but Peril didn't recognize the voice. "First you tell us you're harboring a violent, bloodthirsty criminal, and then you show us a dragonet who has died in *exactly* the way that *creature* kills."

Oh — that's me, Peril realized. *I'm the violent, bloodthirsty criminal. Unfair! I don't thirst for blood. If I need to fry someone to cinders, I will, but I'm not rampaging around killing dragons for fun! I haven't even killed anyone in months! Bloodthirsty INDEED.*

"It was a fire," Tsunami's voice interjected. "I don't like Peril any more than you do, but I promise she didn't do this to Carnelian."

Very supportive, thanks, Tsunami.

The unfamiliar SkyWing hissed with disbelief. "What sounds more likely to you," he snarled, "that Scarlet's pet monster has murdered a dragon loyal to Queen Ruby, or that some MudWing figured out how to set off a dragonflame bomb and accidentally killed our soldier instead of her supposed IceWing target?"

"I want to know where the MudWing is." Queen Ruby's voice was unreadable without her facial expression. Was that cold fury, or grief, or calm decisive leadership? Peril had no idea. This queen was so different from the submissive daughter she'd played all of Peril's life. Peril couldn't figure her out at all.

"You don't seriously believe them?" the other SkyWing cried, his voice rising again. "Look at Carnelian! Look at these burns! Here and here, these marks even look like talon prints!"

Peril coiled into herself, remembering the weight of the dragonet she'd dragged out of the burning cave. Too late, too late to save her. But if she had — if it had worked, if Carnelian were alive now — would Ruby have forgiven her? Would Clay have been proud of her?

Would he have called her his "wings of fire" again, and would it have changed anything?

"Don't touch the body," the queen said sharply.

"Peril pulled Carnelian out of the fire," Sunny said, her voice more subdued than usual. "So you will find Peril's prints on her — but it's because she was trying to save her."

Multiple hostile snorts. The arguing SkyWing clearly wasn't the only one suspicious of the true story.

"Tell me what you're doing to find and punish the MudWing who did this," said Queen Ruby. "What is her name?"

"Sora." That was Clay! It felt like wings spreading inside her heart. Clay was speaking! In his wonderful warm voice! "She — she's my sister."

He sounded so, so sad. Peril wanted to burst into the cave and wrap her wings around him. No, that would only hurt him more. What she should do instead was wrap her wings around the SkyWings who were being mean to him. Then she could watch them burn between her claws.

Now *that* was the kind of thought she probably shouldn't share with Clay.

"Your sister?" said one of the other SkyWings. "This escape is looking more and more convenient, isn't it?"

"Queen Moorhen has agreed to meet with you," Sunny said a little desperately. "Here or at her palace, whichever you prefer — we can send a messenger to her right now. She wants to help you find justice. We all do."

Peril always thought of Clay's soul as a torch that never went out: burning clear and true all night long. Sunny, on the other talon, was a blaze of warm sunlight — the annoying kind that gave a dragon headaches and made you want to scorch things because STOP SMILING ALREADY THE WORLD IS HORRIBLE GO AWAY.

(Peril knew this was bad. Sunny was the only one of Clay's friends who tried to be nice to Peril, and yet Peril still wanted to push her off a cliff on a daily basis. Sometimes she dreamed that she'd left Sunny in Scarlet's cage and run off with Clay, and at the end he'd turn to her and say, "You were right, we don't need anyone else! Forget all the smiling

SandWings and brave SeaWings and beautiful RainWings we've ever known!" But then, she supposed, he wouldn't be Clay, *her* Clay, who loved his friends so much he kept trying to die for them. That was a plan, by the way, that was never going to happen on Peril's watch.)

"Your Majesty," a new voice cut in suddenly. "Someone is approaching from the north."

"Queen Moorhen?" someone else asked.

"No," said the watcher. "I see orange scales . . ." She trailed off, and in the silence that followed, Peril felt an overwhelming wave of horror surge slowly, inexorably toward them and then crash over everyone listening.

"It's Queen Scarlet," Ruby whispered. "You were right. She's still alive."

And coming to kill you, I bet, Peril thought. *Since I wouldn't do it for her.*

It was the night after Peril had freed Scarlet from Burn's weirdling tower. The two of them were huddled around a fire in the unfriendly wasteland between the Ice Kingdom and the Kingdom of Sand. Scarlet was picking bits of reindeer out of her teeth and Peril was trying not to stare at her queen's newly disfigured face.

"We'll go home tomorrow," Scarlet growled. "I'll figure out

how to kill those prophecy brats from there, with or without you."

"You should know —" Peril hesitated.

"What?" Scarlet threw a hoof at her, whacking Peril hard just above her eyes. "Don't mumble! I'm furious at you already! I cannot handle you being annoying as well as disobedient right now!"

Peril rubbed her forehead and tried to remember why she'd thought rescuing Scarlet was a good idea. Or maybe she'd always known it was a bad idea, but she'd still felt as though it was her responsibility. Or maybe she'd just needed Scarlet to stop slithering through her dreams, making every night even worse than the days of crocodile throwing and dragons screaming at her.

"It's just that Ruby is queen now," Peril said. "And the SkyWings really love her," she added, a little vindictively.

Scarlet flapped one dismissive wing. "I know about that. But Ruby will roll right over and hand back my throne. She's a good daughter, unlike SOME dragons I could mention."

"I don't think she will," Peril said. "She's made a lot of changes already. She doesn't do what Burn wants her to do. She's pulled back on all the fronts of the war since destroying the Summer Palace. As if she's consolidating her power and gathering her warriors to defend the palace — and herself.

Plus, she, um . . . she banished me. She's a lot scarier than I thought she was. A lot scarier than you *think* she is."

Scarlet glowered at Peril, her yellow eyes full of flames. After a long moment, she said, "That's what Burn thought, too. That if I tried to return, Ruby would defeat me." She threw back her head and laughed a strange hollow cackle. "Ruby, of all dragons? She's a mouse."

"She's not," Peril said. Truthfully, Peril wasn't sure what Ruby was. But a part of her knew she was digging in her claws about it because she wanted to hurt Scarlet. She wanted to hurt her the way she'd been hurt, and she wanted to scare Scarlet away from the Sky Palace.

True, if Scarlet returned to the Sky Palace, then Peril could, too. She'd have a home again. But it wouldn't be worth it, because then Clay would be in danger. The minute Scarlet had her army back, she'd go after him, and Peril wouldn't be able to stop her.

Scarlet unconsciously reached one talon toward her scarred face, but didn't touch it. "You think Ruby would fight me?" she asked. "She couldn't win. Not against *me*." But Peril could see it in her eyes — Scarlet knew what it was like to be afraid now. The venom attack had melted more than her scales; it had eaten away some of her confidence. The time she spent trapped in Burn's tower of horrors probably hadn't helped either.

Peril shrugged. "I guess you'll find out."

There was a pause.

"No," Scarlet said. "I have a better idea." She bared her teeth at Peril. "You return to the Sky Palace and kill her before I get there."

"I can't do that!" Peril cried. "I'm not even allowed in the Sky Palace. Ruby said she'd have me executed if I went back."

"She can't have you executed if you kill her first," Scarlet said.

"Well, I'm not going to kill her," Peril said. "You can't make me. You can't make me kill anyone else for you. I'm not that kind of dragon anymore."

Scarlet's eyes narrowed. "Oh, really? You think you've changed so much? I know you. You like killing dragons. You've always liked it. It's one of the things I can stand about you — none of the simpering, moaning guilt another dragon might have. You were born to burn your enemies. And mine. Mostly mine."

"I don't have to be," Peril said stubbornly. "Clay says I can be whoever I want to be." She knew right away that mentioning him was a mistake.

"Oh. That MUDWING," Scarlet snarled.

"He wouldn't like it if I killed Queen Ruby," Peril said. "He wouldn't like me at all if I did that."

"But I won't like you if you don't," Scarlet pointed out.

Peril couldn't believe the stab of dismay that made her feel.

Why did she still care, after everything Scarlet had done to her? Why did she feel suddenly horribly desperate to be Scarlet's favorite pet again?

I don't care. Stop caring!

"Just one more dragon," Scarlet purred. "Kill Ruby for me, and then you can go follow your aggravating mud dragon. It's the least you could do after you wouldn't let me kill that SandWing spitball."

Peril poked her claw into a scorched circle of grass under her talons. This could be a way to please Scarlet and perhaps save Clay as well. Could she bargain Ruby's life for Clay's? Would Scarlet promise to let him live?

But, for one thing, she couldn't trust Scarlet to keep her word, and, for another, Clay still wouldn't like it. Even if she only did it to protect him, she knew he'd be disappointed in her. The last time they'd seen each other he'd been hopeful . . . he could see another possible future for her. She wanted to be that dragon for him.

"No," she said. "That's my final answer."

"Then you're useless to me," Scarlet hissed furiously.

The next morning, Scarlet was gone. Peril had not been able to find her, and no one else had seen her for months, even in their dreams . . . until she tried to get an IceWing student to kill the dragonets for her.

Still trying to make other dragons do her killing. So something had kept her scared — maybe Peril's words, or maybe hearing what had happened to Burn and Blister.

But if she was coming this way now, then she wasn't scared anymore. Or perhaps her rage had finally surpassed her fear.

Who was she looking for? Did she know Peril was here?

"I'll go face her," Ruby said, her voice clear and strong.

"No!" cried one of the SkyWings. "We'll fight her off! All of us!"

"That's right," said another. "She's not a challenger — you don't have to face her alone."

"She's an enemy," said a third. "And you're a much better queen than she was. We want you, not her."

"I agree," said Clay. "The throne is yours now and she can't have it back. We'll all fight beside you."

A long pause. Peril stabbed at a crack in the rock wall beside her, scowling. She didn't like the sound of Clay acting all loyal and supportive to someone who wasn't her. That was *her* special Clay voice; that's the one he used when he told Peril she would always have a place at Jade Mountain and said things like "I want you to stay." He wasn't supposed to use it WILLY-NILLY on dragons who hated her.

Ruby cleared her throat. "Thank you," she said. "If that's how you all feel, then we'll fly out there together."

Peril heard claws scraping on the rocks. She pictured the queen spinning toward the sky. A moment later, the cave echoed with the sound of flapping wings as they all took off.

Two SkyWing queens who both dislike me quite a lot.

I should hide. I should run. I should run and hide.

But if Scarlet was out there — and Clay was flying toward her . . .

Peril couldn't let him face her alone.

Scarlet was still her responsibility.

She darted into the cave, barreling past Turtle.

"Where are you going?" he called. "What happened to stealth?"

"I have to protect Clay!" she called back, spreading her wings. She couldn't hear his answer over her wingbeats as she shot through one of the skylights.

It *was* Scarlet. Peril recognized the curve of her wings instantly, and she could see the dark scar on the side of her face even from a distance. The former SkyWing queen was beating her way toward them, her whole body radiating fury and vengeance. Ruby and her soldiers were forming into a defensive wing to confront her.

Peril spiraled up into the clouds and hovered above the mountain peak indecisively. Should she fly down to join the soldiers around Queen Ruby and Clay? What if her appearance sent them into a panic or distracted them from fighting Scarlet? As long as Clay was not in immediate danger, maybe she should wait to see what happened before joining in.

Why was Scarlet even here? She couldn't be planning to attack Jade Mountain all by herself, could she?

Perhaps this had something to do with the students who'd gone looking for her.

A group of four dragonets had gone in search of Scarlet about a week ago, right after Carnelian died. Peril knew from Clay that they'd been in the rainforest with Glory for a day, and then they'd flown away to find an IceWing that Scarlet supposedly had imprisoned somewhere.

But no one knew if they'd found Scarlet, and Peril sort of expected that if they had, they'd all be dead.

Was that why Scarlet was here?

Had the dragonets done something to push her over the edge, from caution to rage?

She felt a sudden compression of alarm in her chest.

Scarlet was carrying something in her claws.

It was too small to be a body, surely . . .

Scarlet wheeled about in the air suddenly, out of flaming distance of the wall of SkyWing soldiers facing her.

"Traitors!" she shrieked. "All of you! Disloyal cowards!" She lifted whatever she was holding and shook it at them. "I destroy anyone who opposes me! I *will* have my vengeance and I *will* get my throne back! This is just one of the dragons I'll kill — and you'll all be next!"

She flung the object at them as hard as she could, then abruptly whirled around and flew away, her enormous wings eating up the distance with powerful strokes.

One of the SkyWings lunged forward to catch the missile.

Peril couldn't hold back her curiosity. She swooped closer as the SkyWing looked down at the thing in his talons, then turned, shuddering, to show it to Ruby and the others.

Sunny began to scream as though her heart was being ripped out of her chest. Clay reached to catch her before she fell out of the sky.

The SkyWing was holding the severed head of Queen Glory of the RainWings.

CHAPTER 3

Tsunami's roar should have flattened the mountains and ripped holes in the sky. She shot after Queen Scarlet, a blue blur against the clouds.

"Go with her!" Queen Ruby shouted at her soldiers. She grabbed the head from the dazed SkyWing who held it. "All of you! Go now!"

They obeyed in one glittering mass of red and orange, except for one who turned at the last minute to face Ruby.

"If we catch her," he said hesitantly, "do you want to — do you want us to —"

"Yes, kill her," Ruby said. "I don't mind who does it."

He nodded and wheeled around to follow the others.

Should I go with them? Peril wondered. Surely there were enough dragons chasing Scarlet without her. What she really wanted to do was take care of Clay. Knowing how he was about his friends . . . Peril guessed, with a stab of jealousy that she was immediately ashamed of, that he must be devastated.

Would he be devastated if that was my *head?*

Stop thinking about yourself, Peril. Worry about Clay.

He was half carrying Sunny down to a flat shelf of gray rock that angled out of the mountain below them. Ruby glanced at the head in her talons and then followed.

So this would be awkward. But it was clearly an emergency. Ruby would just have to deal with Peril's presence, and if she didn't like it, it was her own fault for standing so close to Clay when he was clearly suffering and needed Peril.

Peril dropped out of the sky, landing with a thump in front of Clay and Sunny.

Sunny was sobbing too hard to notice her, and at first, Clay didn't seem to see her either. His brown eyes stared blankly down at the little SandWing, as if his brain had been incinerated.

So it was only Ruby who reacted immediately, recoiling with a hiss of fury at the sight of Peril.

"What are you doing here?" Ruby demanded. "In *my* mountains?"

"These are my friends," Peril said, lifting her chin. "You can't make me stay away from my friends."

"Monsters don't have friends," hissed Ruby.

Peril gave Clay a sideways glance, waiting for him to say something like "she's not a monster!" or "we are her friends!" but he still wasn't even looking at her.

"How could she have killed *Glory*?" Sunny cried. "Glory's amazing and indestructible and has magical death spit plus Deathbringer and a whole army of RainWings who would die for her! Clay, please, *please* tell me that's not her."

"Maybe it's a trick," Clay said, turning numbly toward the head in Ruby's talons.

It didn't look like a trick to Peril. That was definitely the head of the RainWing queen. Peril remembered Glory clearly from her time in the Sky Palace, before she venomed Queen Scarlet. She also remembered her on the sands of Burn's stronghold, holding Clay down while Peril burned out the snakebite poison in his leg.

She was the one who ruined Scarlet's face. The one Scarlet hated the most.

But you'll be next, she thought, glancing at Ruby. *And then . . . maybe me.*

Or maybe the other dragons from the prophecy. Was Clay on Scarlet's list? If she dared . . . if she came anywhere *near* him . . . Peril felt molten lava rippling under her scales and curled in her tail with a soft growl.

Clay's big MudWing wings trembled as he tried to reach out and touch the severed head. If only she could do it for him! Then she could examine it and tell him the horrible truth . . . but she couldn't touch it at all, or it would turn to charred black cinders in her claws.

"It looks like Queen Glory to me," said Ruby. "I'm sorry for you both."

Sunny broke down, covering her face with her talons and curling into a ball with her wings over her head. Clay closed his eyes and his head dropped.

"Can I see?"

Peril and Ruby both looked up and found Turtle flapping down from the sky. He landed and carefully took the head from Ruby, studying it from all sides.

"Who are you?" Ruby asked. "Did you know Queen Glory?"

"No, I never met her," he said. "I'm one of the sons of Queen Coral, and a student here. But I feel like . . . I don't know, just . . . there's something strange about this."

"It is weird," Peril agreed. "Glory was probably the best-guarded dragon in Pyrrhia. How did Scarlet get to her? Why go for her first? Killing Ruby first would make much more sense; then she could have taken the whole SkyWing army to attack the rainforest."

"That's *Queen* Ruby to you," the red dragon snarled. "And I'm not that easy to kill either. No matter who you are or what your claws can do."

Peril glared back at her.

Turtle squinted and held the head up toward the light. "Does she have something in her ear?" He tilted it toward Ruby, enough so that Peril could see a flash of yellowy white tucked inside the dragon's ear.

"A message?" Ruby guessed, taking it back from him. "More threats?"

With careful claws, Turtle reached into the ear canal and slid out a small rolled-up scrap of paper.

As he lifted it out, *Glory's head began to move.*

The scales started rippling as though they were flipping over, from emerald green to brown. The snout widened and the brow went flat and the venomous fangs slid into the gums and vanished.

Ruby shrieked and dropped the head on the ground, where it bounced and rolled to a stop near Peril's talons.

She peered down into a face that was now most definitely a MudWing and not Glory at all.

What in the name of all the moons . . .

Clay grabbed Sunny and nearly lifted her off the ground as he turned her to look.

"What happened?" he cried. "What happened to Glory?"

"Who is *that*?" Ruby demanded.

"Not Queen Glory after all," said Turtle. "This is magic — an enchantment of some kind." He held up the unrolled scrap of paper, then brought it close to his nose to read it aloud. *"Enchant this piece of scroll so that whichever dragon wears it tucked inside his or her ear shall look exactly like Glory of the RainWings."*

There was a long, confused silence.

"It's not Glory," Sunny whispered, exhaling. "Clay! Glory's still alive!"

"Alive," Clay said. His whole face glowed with relief. "But we have to warn her that Scarlet's definitely going after her." He took a deep breath, his wings drifting down like falling leaves. "I wonder who this was," he said softly, nodding at the head.

"Was Scarlet trying to trick you?" Turtle puzzled. "But why? I mean, you'd have figured out the truth sooner or later, once you heard from Glory."

"No," Peril said. "It wasn't about tricking them. She just wanted to scare them. That's her favorite kind of power."

Ruby let out a hiss, and Peril met her eyes.

She saw it then: the new queen was scared of her mother — as scared of her as Peril was.

But Peril caught a glimpse of something else, something bitter and deep inside Ruby that had to do with Peril herself. She curled her talons in.

She'd been thinking of the ways Scarlet always terrified her . . . not all the ways Scarlet had used *her* to terrify others.

Ruby's dark red wings flapped open and closed, like a rug briskly thrown over a body. "Wait," she said. "An enchantment? Doesn't that mean that Scarlet must have an animus?"

"No," Sunny said, stretching her neck uneasily. "*No.* We'd all be dead already if that were true."

Turtle pointed the piece of paper at the MudWing's head. "But . . . uh . . . what else is this?"

Ruby whipped around suddenly to glare at Peril. "*You* must know. Is there an animus dragon working for her?"

"Why would I know?" Peril demanded. *Argh, it would be so SATISFYING to just STOMP on this dragon's tail and watch it burst into flames.* "She didn't tell me things! I was her — her weapon, not her friend. *You're* her daughter, why don't *you* know?"

"No one can stop an animus," said Clay. "Right? Except another animus." He exchanged a glance with Sunny that looked aggravatingly stuffed with secrets.

What was that? Do they know an animus? Why do they have secrets I don't know about? Doesn't Clay know he can tell me anything?

Peril flicked her tail irritably and Ruby leaped away from her, even though her tail hadn't been anywhere *near* the queen's precious scales.

"I thought the SkyWings didn't have any animus dragons," Turtle said. "Not for hundreds of years, if ever."

"Not just SkyWings," said Ruby. "None of the tribes. Animus dragons are so rare — I don't think there's been one in Pyrrhia in centuries."

The next pause had an extremely strange awkwardness to it. Peril glanced from Clay to Turtle to Sunny and realized they *all* knew something she and Ruby didn't.

"What?" Peril demanded. "What is it?"

"Um — my father," Sunny said quickly. "Stonemover . . . he's an animus."

"The old NightWing who lives under this mountain?" Turtle asked. Judging from his tone of surprise, that wasn't the secret he'd been thinking of. Peril wondered if she could threaten it out of him later.

Wait, no. This was one of those things Clay had to remind her about sometimes. Apparently, friends didn't threaten to set each other on fire. Not very often anyhow.

"Yes," Sunny admitted. "He made the tunnels that lead from the rainforest to the NightWing island and the Kingdom of Sand. But he doesn't use his powers anymore."

"He might have to," Ruby said, "if there's a new animus

on the loose, working for Scarlet, and he's the only one who can stop her."

"Could it be another NightWing?" Turtle guessed. "Someone who escaped the volcanic island and went to team up with Scarlet?"

Clay shuddered. "That would be . . . not great for us."

"I'm not afraid of any animus," Peril blurted. "I bet I could stop it — him, her, whatever. I just have to sneak up on them and then POW, brain melted, claws a pile of cinders! No more creepy enchantments. Everybody cheers!" *For me. Everybody cheers for me. Or at least, Clay tells me I'm wonderful.*

Clay didn't have his "you're wonderful" face on, though. He looked all troubled and worried instead.

"But it might not be a bad dragon," Sunny said. "This animus could be someone Scarlet has tricked or forced into working for her. We shouldn't just kill them without knowing the whole story."

"This is definitely not me agreeing with *her*," Ruby said, flicking her tail at Peril, "but I think we absolutely should. Animus dragons are so dangerous — and more so the more they use their powers. According to our history, the SkyWing tribe used to kill them the moment we figured out what they were."

"But —" Sunny looked aghast, as did Turtle. "You mean,

when they were still dragonets? Before they'd even done anything?"

"Before they *could* do anything," Ruby said. "That's our policy with all dragons who are too dangerous to live." She slid her narrowed eyes over to Peril, who had already figured out the subtext of this conversation, thanks very much.

"Oh, dear," Sunny said in a small voice.

"That's not fair," Turtle protested. "Animus dragons can maybe do good things, too."

"Let's save worrying about it until we know she really has one," Clay said. "And who it is. We have enough else to worry about already."

"Like the rest of my winglet," Turtle said, lowering his head. "Do you think Moon and the others are safe? Weren't they going after Scarlet?"

"They were, but I don't know what's happened," Sunny said, pressing her claws together anxiously. "I tried to dreamvisit Kinkajou and Qibli last night but couldn't get into either of their dreams. I haven't been able to since they left. Oh, I hope they're all right."

"They probably are," Peril said. "Or else Scarlet would have been throwing *their* heads at you."

She'd thought that would be very reassuring, but for some reason it made Sunny look even more ill.

"Someone's coming back," Clay said, standing up and spreading his wings to catch the attention of the dragons in the sky.

Three of Ruby's soldiers swooped down, spiraling gracefully until they spotted Peril, at which point they all started flapping like insane pigeons on fire, until they finally landed in a thumping row between her and Ruby.

"Don't you come near our queen," one of them snarled.

"I wasn't *planning* on it," Peril snapped back. "Do you actually think you could stop me if I was?"

"Peril," Clay said softly, warningly.

BLAH. It wasn't FAIR that they could be rude and she couldn't set them on fire, or even growl back at them. But Peril bit her tongue, sat back, and folded her wings across her chest, making sure she took up as little of the space on the rock ledge as possible. Clay gave her a sweet, grateful smile, which almost made it OK.

"Ignore her," Ruby ordered her guards. "What happened?"

"We overtook the SeaWing, but couldn't find Scarlet," said the tall orange soldier. "The rest are still looking, but we wanted to come back and make sure you were guarded, in case it was a trick."

"It was, in a way," said Ruby, nodding at the head.

"Someone has to catch Tsunami," said Sunny. "We have to tell her it's not Glory."

"She," Clay said. "*She* was somebody, even if she's not Glory." He took a deep breath and picked up the head. Peril wished she could turn it to ashes; she didn't like the way the dead brown eyes were staring at her. Piles of ashes were much tidier and less horrifying than stray body parts.

"Wait. If we can figure out who she is and where she's from," Ruby said suddenly, "it might be a clue about where Scarlet is hiding."

"You're right. Let's take her to Queen Moorhen." Clay turned toward Ruby, wincing as he set his weight on his injured leg. "That's the best place to start."

She nodded, tilting her diamond-shaped head toward the orange dragon. "Go catch the SeaWing and tell her to return," she ordered. "My soldiers should split up — half keep looking for Scarlet and the other half return to me. We'll leave for Moorhen's palace at midnight."

All the SkyWings whirled into the air; the orange soldier went north, while Queen Ruby and the other two swept south toward Jade Mountain.

"I'm going to try the dreamvisitor again," Sunny said to Clay.

He reached over and twined his tail around hers, and Peril felt a stab of jealousy so fierce she was surprised flames didn't come shooting out of her eyeballs.

"They're all right. I'm sure they are," Clay said quietly to Sunny.

She shook her head without answering and lifted off into the sky.

Only Clay and Peril were left on the ledge. At last. She gazed deep into his warm brown eyes . . .

"So, Scarlet is pretty scary, huh?"

Oh, right, and Turtle. The SeaWing edged closer to them, twitching his wings curiously.

Peril tried giving him a significant look, of the go-away-we're-having-a-moment variety, but he didn't seem to notice.

"Yes, she is," Clay said with a sigh.

What kind of sigh was that? Peril wondered. *Was it an "I wish I were alone with Peril" sigh? Or a "worried about my students" sigh?* Knowing Clay, it could also be a "we're all out of goats and I really wanted one" sigh.

"What are *you* going to do?" she asked him.

"I should stay here and guard the academy," he said thoughtfully. "But if Ruby agrees to leave enough guards to protect the students, I might go with her to see Queen Moorhen."

Peril didn't like that plan. She had a feeling she wouldn't be invited along on any diplomatic missions, especially any that involved going inside other queens' palaces and possibly incinerating their national treasures by accident or whatever.

"What about me?" she asked. "What should I do?"

He gave her a rueful smile that lit candles in her heart. "Whatever you want to do, Peril. That's the whole point of being free from Scarlet, isn't it?"

"But what do you want me to do?" she pressed.

"Peril," Clay said, "I'm not going to be a new Scarlet for you. You get to make your own choices now."

I am making my own choices, Peril thought grumpily. *I'm choosing to do whatever you think I should do.*

Maybe she could figure out what he wanted from the clues. Sometimes when Queen Scarlet was really angry, she wouldn't speak to Peril for weeks, and then Peril had to figure out on her own what she'd done wrong and how to fix it to make Queen Scarlet happy again.

So . . . what did Clay want?

She studied him from horns to tail. He had turned to gaze back at Jade Mountain, his wings drooping heavily.

All right, it was pretty obvious: he wanted his friends and his school to be safe.

And the only way to do *that* was to get rid of Queen Scarlet forever.

Peril inhaled a sharp breath. That was it. Clay would never say it out loud — he'd never ask her for it directly. But what he really wanted her to do was find Queen Scarlet and kill her for him.

She might be the only dragon in Pyrrhia who could —
especially if an animus was protecting Scarlet now.

So as much as she never, never wanted to see Scarlet again,
and as much as the idea of leaving Clay to find her was heart-
wrenching, that was what she was going to have to do.

It's all right, Clay, she thought. *You don't have to tell me. I
know what you want, and I'll do it for you.*

I'll find Queen Scarlet.

And I'll make sure she never ever hurts you again.

CHAPTER 4

The plan was to sneak away in the middle of the night. That sounded like something a hero would do. She would set off on her quest alone, boldly but quietly, without giving anyone a chance to talk her out of it.

Peril could imagine flying bravely into the night — and even better than that, she could imagine the scene the next morning, when Clay found her gone and threw back his head and cried "Noooo! Peril! She's gone to save us all! She's so noble and self-sacrificing! But what am I going to do without her? Oh, the unbearable pain!!"

But here was the problem: when she kept going with that scene in her head, the next thing that happened was Sunny or Tsunami or Starflight showing up. And then one of them would say something like "Or hey, maybe she's run off because she's actually evil and in cahoots with Scarlet after all," and/or "I knew we couldn't trust her!"

And it all went downhill from there.

Peril didn't want to leave Clay wondering what she was really up to. She didn't care what the others thought of her, but in all the world, Clay was the only dragon who saw more good in her than bad. She didn't want him to have even a moment of "is Peril really as dangerous and unstable as everyone's been telling me?"

So clearly she had to say good-bye to him. That was obvious. It wasn't just that she wanted to see him one more time. Or that she was hoping he'd tell her not to go. No, no, none of those. It was for his own sake, really.

She waited until the halls were quiet, and then she slipped out of her sleeping cave, which was as bare and empty as the day she'd stepped into it. Everyone else in the school had to share their sleeping cave — but then, no one else could accidentally burn up her clawmates just by rolling over in the middle of the night.

Clay had offered Peril a cave closer to the other students, but he'd seemed relieved when she refused it. So hers was close to the dragonets who ran the school instead — but she still had to go through the main central cave to get to Clay.

Which is where she nearly ran into Turtle for the second time that day.

Seriously, if a dragonet insisted on flopping like a lumpy boulder in the middle of a dimly lit cave, wasn't it *his own fault* if he got set on fire?

"AAAAH! Why are you always in the WAY?" she demanded, backpedaling at the last minute to avoid stepping on his talons.

"Am I?" he said sleepily, lifting his head. "I'm not usually. I don't think. Other dragons go around me or over me pretty well."

"You won't be pleased if *I* go over you," Peril pointed out. "Why aren't you in your own sleeping cave?"

Turtle gave a little shiver. "It feels weird in there now that Umber is gone. And all the rest of my winglet, too. I should have gone with them," he mumbled.

"Not if they're all dead now," Peril said sensibly. "If Scarlet has killed them, then staying here was obviously the smart choice."

He sat up fast, and Peril tilted her head, trying to read his expression. Alarmed or horrified? Anxiety? Guilt? All of the above?

"*No,*" Turtle protested. "Are you crazy? That would be even worse! What if you're right and they're dead and I could have saved them?"

"Really? You?" Peril said.

"I do not APPRECIATE your skeptical tone," he said, sounding briefly like an actual prince. "Just because I don't particularly like danger or uncertainty or . . . or *exercise* . . . doesn't mean I couldn't be useful in a fight."

Peril paused, trying to figure out how to say what she wanted to say without the skeptical tone. "RrrrrrEEEally?" she tried, infusing the word with as much enthusiastic curiosity as she could. "YOUUUUUUU?"

Turtle burst out laughing. "You're so weird," he said.

"I'm not the one sleeping in the entrance hall," Peril said. "Asking to get trampled and scorched."

"Well, the other thing is that Tsunami isn't back yet," he admitted. "I'm sort of waiting for her."

"Uh-oh," Peril said. He gave her an anxious look and she added quickly, "I mean, that probably doesn't mean anything. Anything involving decapitation, that is."

"You have this uncanny ability to say whatever is the opposite of comforting," he observed wryly.

"That wasn't comforting?" she asked. "Um . . . how about, I'm sure she's fine because a SeaWing dragonet like her could never possibly catch up with a full-grown SkyWing like Scarlet. Oh, unless it was a trap and Scarlet ambushed her."

Turtle wrinkled his snout at her and Peril shifted on her talons. "OK, I know, I heard it that time. But it was a smart thought, wasn't it?"

He turned to look out at the stars. "So what do we do?" he asked. "Send more dragons to look for her? What if Scarlet ambushes everyone? We don't know how many dragons she might have working for her. What if this is her plan, and she kills everyone we send after Tsunami?"

"She can't kill *me*," Peril pointed out. "I'd like to see her try! Ha!"

Turtle gave her an odd, glittering look. "You're right," he said. "You and me. We should go."

"That's what I — wait, no," she said. "What? She can definitely kill *you*."

"Maybe not," he said. "Anyway, Tsunami's my sister. And my winglet is out there somewhere —"

"You hope," Peril interjected. "Er . . . I mean, YES, they ARE."

Turtle lifted one of his wings to shush her, tilting his head. "Someone's coming," he whispered. "Hide!" He ran over to the enormous gong in the center of the hall and dove behind it.

Startled, Peril twisted around in a circle before she found a shadowy corner where there was an outgrowth of stalagmites to hide behind. She tucked herself into the darkness and whispered loudly, "Why are we hiding?"

"*SHHHH*," Turtle answered.

Peril tried to remember the last time she'd ever hidden from anyone before she'd met Turtle. Maybe in the Kingdom of Sand, when she was trying to sneak up on Burn's stronghold to rescue Scarlet. But hiding was not normally her approach to problems. Why hide when you could always set your problem on fire?

Now she could hear voices approaching. One of them sounded like Clay, who was exactly the dragon she was looking for. Except now if she popped out of her hiding place he'd be, like, "um, what were you doing back there?" and it would look so, so weird and maybe suspicious, too. ARRRRGH.

Thanks a lot, Turtle. *What is with this dragon and the eavesdropping?*

"Ten soldiers should be enough to guard this place," Ruby's voice said. Peril heard three sets of talons enter the cave, and she pressed herself closer to the floor. "And with luck we'll be back in three days. I don't want to be away from the Sky Palace for too long. I have . . . someone waiting for me."

"Thank you, Queen Ruby." That was Starflight, the NightWing librarian.

"Did your student tell you anything else we should know?" Ruby asked. "Apart from the disturbing news about my mother's new ally?"

"Not much," Clay said with a sigh. "Moon's in Possibility, with Qibli. Sunny is dreamvisiting with Glory now, so she can send someone up to the town to take care of Kinkajou."

"Poor Kinkajou," Starflight said softly.

Uh-oh, Peril thought. She had seen the bouncy little RainWing from a distance, but mostly she'd only heard about her from Clay. If she was hurt, he must be upset. And what had happened to the other missing dragonet, Winter? The IceWing who hated her? Peril would be all right with him being dead, out of the four dragonets. But Clay wouldn't, of course. He'd feel all responsible and protective and worried. Oh dear, was he all right? She wished she could see his face.

"One last word of warning, although I know you won't listen to me," Ruby said, stopping with a loud swish of her tail. "You cannot trust my mother's creature. She's unpredictable and knows nothing but killing. If you won't banish her, at least don't leave her unguarded for an instant."

"I can trust Peril," Clay said, and in her shadows Peril felt her entire soul turn into a fireball. "She saved my life."

"Plus she's in love with Clay," Starflight added.

Peril wondered if anyone would notice if she flew over, ripped out his tongue, and vanished into the night sky forever.

"Ack!" Clay said. "Three moons, Starflight! That's not — it's not even — we're — no, no, no. I trust her because there's good in her, and we just need to give her a chance to show it to us."

"She may have a fragment of good in her somewhere," Ruby said doubtfully, "but she'll never be good enough for you. And if he's right, and if she ever thinks you don't love her back, she will set all your friends on fire. That's just the truth."

"Um," said Starflight. "For the record, I don't like the sound of that at all."

Peril closed her eyes. *Was* it true? What would happen if Clay didn't love her? Or if he ever tried to send her away? It was a horrible, soul-crushing thought. But she wouldn't really set his friends on fire, would she?

Not *all* of them anyway.

No, she told herself severely. *None of them. Not even if it's their fault he doesn't love me.* Oooorgh, but what if Tsunami convinced him to get rid of her? She might totally do something like that. Then could Peril set just the tiniest part of her on fire?

No, no, no. Because there's always the chance he might *still love me one day, but he definitely won't if there's any friend-burning at all.*

"Let's not talk about this," Clay said awkwardly. "Your Majesty, I'll meet you back here at midnight."

"All right, well," she said. "You've been warned." She swept majestically out of the cave, her tail making quiet dramatic swishing noises against the stone floor.

"Should I be worried?" Starflight asked. "Am I going to wake up on fire one day? How worried should I be?"

"Not at all," Clay said. "Peril is not going to set you on fire."

"I wonder if I have any scrolls about sociopaths," Starflight muttered.

"Stop that." Clay stamped one of his feet. "I'm going to ask Sunny to dreamvisit Tsunami and see if she can find her."

"Queen Ruby will never believe Peril has changed," Starflight called after him. There was a pause as Clay's footsteps faded away. "Not sure we will either," he added to himself, and then Peril heard his talons scrape against the rock as he bustled off to the library.

Silence fell across the cavern.

Peril curled her claws in and took a deep breath.

"Sorry about that," Turtle said, his voice whispering across the empty space. A few moments later, his head popped around the edge of the rocks she was hiding behind. "I've been doing that all my life and I've never heard anyone say anything about me."

"That's because you're boring and forgettable," Peril snapped.

"I know," he said unexpectedly. "I try to be."

"Well, I don't have that option," she said, spreading her smoking talons. "ROAR. This would be a really good time to have a dungeon full of enemies."

"What?" he said. "Why?"

"Because," she said, "when you're mad, it's useful to have dragons around that you can set on fire without getting in trouble."

He rolled his eyes. "Somehow, I don't think Clay and Starflight would be pleased if you set anyone on fire, even their enemies."

"That makes no sense," Peril said. "Everyone wants to see their enemies on fire. Are you telling me your mother never cheered herself up by having someone torch a bunch of bad guys in front of her?"

"Um, no," said Turtle. "First of all, we're SeaWings, so we don't have fire, remember? Secondly, my mother mostly cheered herself up by writing scrolls about all her problems. And third, she used her prisoners as bargaining chips, not toys."

"Our prisoners were definitely Scarlet's toys," Peril said.

"And so were you, it sounds like."

Peril snorted a burst of flame and he jumped back. "No! I was more than that! I was like a daughter to her!"

"All right, all right," he said. "So what are you going to do about Ruby and Clay and all of that?"

"What can I do?" she said. "You heard Starflight. They'll never trust me with Clay. And they're right: I'm *not* good enough for him. He's good all the way through, not just in little fragments. I mean, if saving Clay's life wasn't enough, what else is there?"

"I can think of one thing," he said. "I bet it would make everyone forgive you, even Ruby."

"Well," Peril said. "Yes. I thought of that."

"You have to kill Queen Scarlet," he said. "And I'm coming with you."

CHAPTER 5

The clouds swept past them like ribbons of smoke, sliced and scattered by the slash of their wings. Below them, the Claws of the Clouds Mountains lurked like the long, long spine of a giant sleeping dragon, black except where the craggy peaks were studded with light from the moons. Peril could see the silver flicker of the Winding Tail River running along the eastern edge of the mountain range. They were about to fly over the curve where it veered east and then north again.

She loved flying, and not just because she was a SkyWing and all SkyWings loved to fly. It was more than that for her. There was nothing else in her life that she could love in such a joyful, uncomplicated way. Up in the sky she could stretch her wings as wide as she wanted; she could whip her tail and dive and soar and spin, and she didn't have to keep all her limbs so carefully close to her, watching her perimeter every moment.

Up here, there was nothing to burn.

Everyone and everything was safe from her as long as she was in the sky. At least, that was usually the case. She didn't normally have a SeaWing flapping around on her tail. He was doing a reasonably good job of keeping his distance, but she felt a startled jolt every time she saw him out of the corner of her eye.

Peril still wished she could have talked to Clay before she left. But she wasn't sure she could look him in the face anymore after the conversation she'd overheard.

Not until I'm bringing him the charred bones of Queen Scarlet anyway.

"Where are we going?" Turtle called from behind her.

She twisted in midair to give him an incredulous look. "To kill Queen Scarlet," she said. "Remember? There was a whole conversation a few hours ago. I'm pretty sure you were there, because I was like, 'you're not coming with me,' and you were all, 'how are you going to stop me?' and I was all, 'I can think of a pretty good way,' and you were like, 'by setting me on fire? That sounds like cutting off your tail to spite your wings,' and I was like, 'I could cut off YOUR tail,' and you were all, 'let's just go before Ruby comes back —' "

"All right," Turtle finally interrupted. "I know all *that*. I mean, *where* are we going to kill Queen Scarlet? How do we even start looking for her? Or my sister?"

"Oh." Peril did a looping flip in the sky. She had searched for Scarlet for months after releasing her from Burn's weirdling tower, with no success. What did she think would be different now?

"The mountains?" she suggested. "Maybe we could . . . fly around them. A lot."

"Forgive me for mentioning this," Turtle said, "but I'm getting the impression that you're not much of a planner."

"What have I ever needed to plan?" Peril demanded. "Do you know anything about my life? Here's how it went: Wake up, eat breakfast, Queen Scarlet tells me to kill one of her prisoners, I kill that prisoner, eat dinner, go back to sleep. Pretty simple. Not a lot of big decision-making involved."

"Really?" Turtle asked. "Were you happy?"

Peril let herself drop to a warmer air current, trying to think. Happy? Was that how she'd felt back then? It was definitely *easier* than life after Queen Scarlet (or rather, life after meeting Clay). In the Sky Palace, she'd had a purpose. There was a reason for her scales to be as deadly as they were. She'd been loyal to the queen, and she'd thought the queen cared about her, too, most of the time. Maybe half the time. Well, some of the time anyhow.

She was probably supposed to say something about how terrible it was to kill all those dragons, how it ate her up inside every night and made her miserable. But it *didn't*. Not back then, not while it was happening. She'd been killing dragons for Queen Scarlet for as long as she could remember. That was just . . . her life.

"I had an idea," Turtle said. "I bet Tsunami will head for water if she's stopped anywhere. Can we check for clues down by the river?"

Peril was too busy thinking to argue with him. She followed him down in a drifting spiral until they reached a rocky spot along the riverbank. Turtle landed in the water with a splash while Peril came down gently on the shore. She'd tried to aim for a spot with nothing but rocks and sand, but her tail accidentally flicked against a small shrub growing near the water. It instantly burst into flames, and almost as quickly burned out into a blackened heap, shriveled branches sticking out of it like skeletal claws.

"Ack," Peril said, curling her tail in. "Sorry."

Turtle blinked at the plant but didn't say anything. He stuck his nose in the river and then shook it, spraying droplets everywhere. A few hit Peril, sizzling on her scales.

"Maybe I wasn't happy," she blurted. He looked startled, and a little confused, as if he'd forgotten what they were talking about. She couldn't stop herself from barreling on, though. "But I also wasn't so worried all the time. I only had one dragon to please, and I didn't always manage that, but at least I understood what I needed to do. Now everything is confusing. I guess — I mean, which would you rather be: lonely or insecure?"

The SeaWing spread his wings across the surface of the water, sending ripples out in all directions. "Well," he said, "I've tried lonely, so maybe I'd pick insecure." He pounced suddenly, sending a cascade of water over Peril's talons, and then sat up, brandishing a fish speared on one of his claws. "Hungry?"

"No, thanks," Peril said. She glanced up and down the river. Two of the moons were up, so she could see the outline of trees on the far side and the small flutterings of owls swooping through, hunting.

Turtle began splashing upriver and Peril followed him, pacing along the riverbank and avoiding anything that looked flammable.

"Maybe we should head to Possibility," Turtle said. "We can meet up with Moon and Qibli there and find out what happened to Winter and Kinkajou." His voice hitched slightly on the last word, and Peril gave him a sharp look.

"What was that?" she demanded. "Are you about to cry?"

"*No,*" he said, biting the head off the fish. "I'm just worried about them."

"They're safer in Possibility than anywhere," Peril said. "It's a town full of dragons and more than half of them aren't too fond of Queen Scarlet. At least, they really, really don't like being asked about her. They tend to throw things. Which they also do when you set even the smallest basket of snails on fire — by accident, mind you. Frankly, I think they should rename the place Unnecessary Violent Overreaction."

In the moonlight, she couldn't tell if Turtle's expression was concerned or mildly amused.

"Anyway," she went on, "I'm not looking for an entourage. If I take more dragons with me to face Queen Scarlet, it just means more dragons for her to kill."

"Is that what you think is going to happen to me?" he asked.

"Probably," she said. "I mean — wait, what's the reassuring thing to say?"

"No," he said. "That one's pretty easy. The correct answer is no."

"Oh," she said. "OK, that."

"But Moon and Qibli might know where Scarlet is," Turtle pointed out. A choir of yawping frogs had been burbling away nearby, but cut off abruptly as the dragons approached. "Ruby said they told Sunny something about a new ally of hers, remember?"

Peril frowned. How could Queen Scarlet have a *new* ally? Who was it, and where did he come from?

Does she like him more than me?

She caught herself with a stamp of annoyance that sent sparks flying off one of the stones underfoot. Of course Scarlet would like her new ally more than Peril — whoever it was must have agreed to help her when Peril wouldn't. Also, more importantly, Peril shouldn't care anymore. It was habit to want Scarlet to like her more than anyone, but it was a *bad* habit, and she wished she could scour it out of her brain.

The new ally — was it an animus dragon? The one who had enchanted the severed head? Did that mean other magic was lurking up ahead for them?

"Um . . . does it seem quieter than it should be?" Turtle asked, pausing in the center of the river. Peril stopped and listened, too. The water shivered softly around Turtle's talons, as if it were trying to echo the rustling leaves in the wind overhead.

But there were no more owls swooping, no frogs glurping. It seemed as though even the insects had fallen silent.

Peril slowly twisted in place, scanning the dark trees, wishing she had night vision.

Was that a glimmer of silver scales off to the left?

Did she just imagine the crack of a branch snapping under talons?

Could she smell a hint of smoke on the air?

And then, all of a sudden, the river exploded.

Turtle let out a yell of fright as three dragons burst out of the water almost directly beneath his talons. They seized his wings and tail and pinned him down with a violent splash that cascaded over Peril's scales.

At the same moment, two more dragons flew out of the forest, their claws outstretched and teeth bared. Peril whirled to face them, flinging her wings open.

Try to grab me! Just try!

A dazzling thrill darted through her like lightning. These dragons were attacking her! She could *totally set them on fire* without getting in trouble!

I'm not being bad, Clay! I'm just defending myself! She flexed her talons and tried to squash her grin.

"Don't touch her!" Turtle bellowed, thrashing around like a vomiting whale. "It'll kill you! Her scales are fire!"

The two dragons skidded to a stop just out of her reach. Their claws left grooves in the pebbled sand and their wings flung a blanket of hot air in her direction.

Way to spoil my fun, Turtle.

Although, yes, fine, warning them was probably the Clay-approved thing to do.

"He's right," she said, glowering at her attackers. "I am Peril of the SkyWings. Perhaps you've heard of me." One of the dragons was a big red SkyWing, and Peril definitely saw her flinch and take a step back. "But if you'd like to find out whether he's telling the truth, come a bit closer and we can do a fun experiment." She spread her wet front talons in front of her and smiled wickedly at the coils of steam still rising from them.

"It's true," said the SkyWing. "I recognize her now. Stay back, Cirrus."

The other dragon, a severe-looking IceWing, gave Peril a scornful look as if he highly doubted anyone, even a fire-scales dragon, could possibly be a match for him.

Oooo, please try it, Peril thought, giving him an innocent expression.

"So it's not Scarlet?" asked one of the SeaWings.

The SkyWing lashed her tail. "No. This is Peril, who might be worse."

"I beg your pardon," said Peril, genuinely offended. "Maybe you haven't heard. I'm friends with the dragonets of destiny now. I don't set other dragons on fire anymore. Not unless they provoke me," she added, shooting the IceWing a fierce glare.

"That is one of the rumors going around," said the SkyWing. "But we all know a dragon can't change her scales."

"Maybe not, but I can change my *mind,*" Peril said defiantly. "Unlike *some* dragons, apparently."

"I've not only heard of you, little monster," said the SkyWing, "I was one of the guards sent after your mother when she tried to escape with you." She took a step toward Peril, lashing her tail and looking murderous.

"Avalanche," one of the SeaWings said softly. "Careful —"

"My biggest regret," said Avalanche, smoke billowing from her mouth and ears, "is that we didn't kill you then. I don't care that Kestrel got away. But if I'd known Scarlet would keep you alive —"

"Wait," said Cirrus, flaring his silver-white wings. "Did you say Kestrel?"

Avalanche gave him an irritated look. "Yes. What?"

"Kestrel of the SkyWings?" Cirrus said. "Big, red, grumpy-looking?"

"You've just described fifty percent of all SkyWings," said the MudWing sitting on top of Turtle. "The other half is big, orange, and grumpy-looking."

"What does she have to do with anything?" Cirrus asked.

"She was this creature's mother," Avalanche said. "The one who wouldn't hand her over to be killed."

Cirrus frowned, carving deep canyons across his forehead. "That can't be right. Kestrel never had any dragonets."

"Ha," Avalanche muttered. "We all wish THAT were true."

"Did you know her?" Peril asked Cirrus. He was shaking his head, but there was something weird in his expression.

"I doubt you would have met," said the SeaWing who'd spoken before. "She joined the Talons of Peace before you did, and then she was assigned to guarding the dragonets underground before you came to us. Once the guardians went into hiding with the eggs, most of the Talons of Peace never saw them."

"But you did?" Peril asked the IceWing again. Cirrus looked as if a pile of ashes was slowly turning back into a dragon right in front of his eyes. But was he happy? Angry? Confused? She couldn't tell what he even thought about Kestrel, although he was clearly feeling *something*.

"No," he said, shaking his head again, more vigorously. "Not — that is, only by reputation."

Peril wondered if he was lying. But how could an IceWing have known her mother, if they didn't meet in the Talons of Peace?

"Can I get back to my menacing story now?" Avalanche demanded.

"Oh, let me skip to the ending," Peril said. "You failed to catch or kill my mother as she escaped. You were punished. Then you discovered that I was still alive, instead of flung off a cliff like most firescales dragonets, and you've been seething about it ever since, which is funny because I have never had even one thought about *you* in my entire life."

Avalanche glowered at her for a long moment. Peril flicked her tail gently, casually, and a clump of reeds burst into flames behind her.

"Oops," she said.

There was something very satisfying about how the SeaWings yelped and went scrambling around, splashing water over the fire with their wings. Of course, Peril had really done it to see that expression of powerless fury on Avalanche's face.

"Are you in league with Scarlet?" one of the SeaWings asked breathlessly when the fire was out. "We heard she was recently seen not far from here. Do you know where she is?"

"No," Peril snapped.

"We're looking for her, too," Turtle offered, his voice muffled by the MudWing tail draped across his face. "I mean," he added hastily, "not to join her. To, uh, kill her and stuff."

We need to have a chat about oversharing, Turtle.

"Who are *you*?" Peril demanded, hoping to turn the tables on them.

"We're from the Talons of Peace — my name is Nautilus," said the green SeaWing who'd done the most talking. "We spotted you flying and we've been tracking you for a while.

There are several groups out looking for an orange SkyWing tonight."

"Since *I'm* clearly not Scarlet," said Turtle's squashed-sounding voice, "is there any chance I could get up now?"

"Oh! Yes, sorry." Nautilus flicked his tail at the other two dragons, motioning them away. The MudWing scowled as she heaved herself off Turtle's wings.

"How did you know Scarlet was around?" Turtle asked, stretching his wings and neck with little crackling noises. "Did someone see her?"

"One of your alleged friends, in fact." Avalanche sneered at Peril.

"Tsunami tried to chase her, but when she lost Scarlet not far from here, she came to the Talons of Peace for extra help." Nautilus puffed up his chest. "With all of us looking, Scarlet won't get far."

"Tsunami is with you?" Turtle blurted. "Where? Can we see her? We have a message for her."

"She's out hunting Scarlet with Riptide and his group right now," Nautilus said haughtily, "but I can pass along anything you want her to know."

"All right, tell her Glory isn't dead," Turtle said. "Tell her it was a trick — it was a different dragon. Glory is fine. You have to tell her that as soon as possible."

Nautilus and Avalanche exchanged glances, and Peril realized that now they believed them. So maybe Turtle's forest fire approach to blathering information was not so terrible, after all.

"I'll go," said the other SeaWing. "I think I know where their patrol went." He spread his wings and took off from the water in one smooth motion, like a small island suddenly whisking into the sky.

Nautilus watched him go, but Peril saw that the IceWing, Cirrus, still had his glittering eyes on her.

"Are you wondering if my fire works on IceWing scales?" she asked him. "The answer is yes, your wings and talons and face will melt and shrivel into ash just like anyone else's. I know from experience."

"We're not going to release them into the wild," Cirrus hissed at the others, ignoring her. "You said it yourself — she's even more dangerous than Scarlet."

"Wow, you have a very confused and amusing view of this situation," Peril said. "We're not your prisoners. You couldn't take me prisoner even with an army of IceWings. Not even if all of them had arrogant foreheads like yours. There isn't actually a world in which you need to decide whether to 'release' me. I released myself a long time ago, but thanks anyway."

She thought she was actually showing remarkably noble restraint here. He was basically *asking* to have his talons scorched off.

"We have no reason to hold them," said Nautilus.

"Especially since you *literally can't*," Peril pointed out. Maybe she needed to set something else on fire to make this point.

"Hey, we're all on the same side here," Turtle said. Avalanche snorted, sending tiny puffs of smoke out of her ears. "We all want to catch Scarlet."

"And where are you going to look for her?" Cirrus demanded.

"We're going to Possibility first," said Turtle.

"Not that it's any of your business," Peril said, giving Turtle a stern look.

"To find our friends," Turtle added, as if stern looks completely meant NOTHING in his universe. "Please tell Tsunami that, too."

"We will," said Nautilus. He nudged one of Turtle's wings with his. It was one of those casual things Peril saw dragons do to other members of their tribes all the time — in this case, it was the kind of touch that she guessed meant, "we're both SeaWings, so in the end we'll stick together."

Nobody had ever nudged Peril that way. Apart from the fact that it would probably kill them, no other SkyWing had ever wanted to acknowledge that they were in the same tribe. There was this whole language of nudges and tail flicks and wing brushing that Peril couldn't speak — except with Clay.

But trying to speak it with Clay made her feel like a dragon with no tongue and no ears. What did it mean when he brushed her wing with his as he went by in the tunnels? Did it mean "I love you as much as you love me even if our deep powerful feelings cannot be expressed aloud"? Or "don't worry, I see how nervous you are, but remember I'm always here to take care of you"? Or "it's a dark world, Peril, but you and I will stand in the fire and be safe, because we have each other"?

Sometimes she worried that it just meant "Hey."

But she couldn't *ask* him. She couldn't let him know that she was even weirder and more confused than he realized.

"Good luck," Nautilus said.

"You too," said Turtle.

"I hope you die," Avalanche said to Peril.

"I would say it's mutual," said Peril, "except that I'm going to forget you exist in about a minute, so I don't actually care."

She was rewarded for that brilliance with another expression of helpless rage. *That's right, you self-righteous fish nose.*

I learned a few things from Queen Scarlet, who could burn dragons without touching them.

Shooting a scornful look at Avalanche and Cirrus, Peril leaped into the sky with Turtle not far behind her.

As she wheeled to fly north, she thought about what she'd said to Avalanche.

"I'll forget you exist in a minute . . . I don't actually care . . ."

If only it were true.

Ice Kingdom

Sky Kingdom

Queen Thorn's
Stronghold

Claws of the
Clouds Mountains

Kingdom of
Sand

Scorpion Den

Jade Mountain

PART TWO

POSSIBILITY

—— CHAPTER 6 ——

They flew north toward Possibility for two days — two days of soaring over the mountains, two days of arguing over whether to even go to Possibility at all, although in the end Peril gave in because she couldn't think of any better ways to track Scarlet.

She quickly learned that Turtle didn't have half the stamina she did for long flights. That was probably a SeaWing-SkyWing thing. Or possibly a Turtle-would-rather-be-napping-than-exercising thing. They had to rest *ridiculously* often. He would find a lake and float around, moaning about his sore wings, while she swooped in ever-widening circles, scanning the ground with sharp eyes.

There was no sign of Scarlet anywhere, though. Once they saw another wing of dragons who were probably from the Talons of Peace, given the different colors of their scales, but it was far off in the distance. Perhaps they'd heard about the encounter by the river, because they didn't come over to investigate Peril.

Peril also spotted several SkyWings spiraling around the mountain peaks. She wondered if Ruby had sent out more soldiers to search for Queen Scarlet. Ruby's throne was in danger now that everyone knew the former queen was definitely alive and out for vengeance. Until someone killed her, Scarlet would always have supporters in the Sky Kingdom. What if one of them decided to kill Ruby on her behalf?

I bet she wishes she'd been nicer to me now. Who'd be a better guard than me? Yes, I'm dangerous; that's exactly what's awesome about me. That's why she needs me. I should be right next to the queen, not banished from the whole smoldering kingdom.

But then, if she'd stayed with Ruby, she couldn't be wherever Clay was.

So I'll do this one thing for Ruby. I'll find Queen Scarlet, turn her into a pile of ashes, get all redeemed and pardoned and welcomed back everywhere, and then return to Clay as a beloved SkyWing who can go anywhere I want . . . and be with anyone I want, because I'll be a hero, too.

Peril did three backward loops in the sky, waiting for Turtle to catch up. She could *see* the rosy, fuzzy glow around the ridiculous fantasy she was building in her head, but she couldn't help it: she still kind of believed it could come true.

Turtle flapped up, panting a little. "I think," he wheezed, "someone might be . . . following us."

"Really?" Peril scanned the horizon behind them. They were out of the mountains now, flying over the rocky sloping hills that led to the river plain and then north to Possibility. The smudge of the town was visible in the distance — they could probably reach it by nightfall. Well, *she* could, if she were flying alone. With a gasping SeaWing on her tail, they'd probably have to sleep on it and get there in the morning.

In any case, the landscape below and behind them was relatively flat compared to the Claws of the Clouds Mountains, so it would be harder for a dragon following them to hide.

"I don't see anything," she said.

"That grove of trees back there." Turtle pointed. "I thought I saw a dragon dive into them when I turned around."

Peril squinted, trying to figure out if she could see wings moving in the scraggly clump of wishful forest. One way to find out, of course, would be to go set the trees on fire. It didn't seem worth the effort, though.

"Was it an orange dragon?" she asked.

"Noooo," Turtle said. "Black, I think."

Peril shrugged. "All right. Whatever." She lifted herself to another current so she could spin around at a safe distance from Turtle and began flying north again.

"Really?" Turtle said, beating his wings to keep up. "We're not worried about that?"

"Why would we be?" Peril asked, amused. "As long as it's not Scarlet, who cares? It's not like anyone can hurt us. Well, me. No one can hurt me. I guess *you* are welcome to worry."

"Oh, thanks very much," Turtle said. "And that's not true — I'm sure dragons can hurt you."

"How?" Peril demanded. "No, they can't! I'm fine as long as I don't listen to them! They're all stupid anyway! Who cares what a bunch of Ruby-butt-noses say; NOT ME, that's for sure. I mean, come over here and say that with my talons up your snout! Ha!"

He gave her an odd look. "Actually, I meant with a spear or frostbreath or something."

"Oh," Peril said. "I guess, maybe. The dragons in the arena never had spears."

"And their wings were bound, so they couldn't fly, right?" Turtle asked.

Peril frowned at him. "I didn't fly while we were fighting either," she said. "That wasn't to make them easier to kill. That was so they wouldn't be boring and run away."

"You mean, be *sensible* and run away," Turtle said. He twisted around to look behind them again. "Nothing. Whoever it is is still hiding."

"Or you hallucinated it," Peril said grumpily. "Frostbreath doesn't do anything to my scales, by the way. And I bet a spear would burn up before it could stab me."

"Not if someone threw it at you really hard," Turtle mused. "Then it would be like, *bam*, spear through the heart, and even if it did then burst into flames, well, too late."

"This conversation is fun," Peril said. "Next let's talk about all the ways *you* could possibly die. I have a few ideas."

"Or if Scarlet has an animus, she could enchant something to kill you," Turtle pointed out. "Then there's nothing you could do about it."

"But if she could do that, Glory really would be dead already," Peril argued. "And Ruby. Those are the two she would start with. I'm only, like, seventh or eighth on her list, probably. So I'm not going to worry about imaginary animus dragons until those guys start turning up dead."

She fell silent abruptly, realizing that Clay was probably in Scarlet's top five on her to-be-murdered list. *Maybe I shouldn't have left him alone. Maybe he's the one I should be guarding all the time . . . day and night . . . never leaving his side . . .*

She let herself imagine that for a while before coming back to reality with a sigh. No, the best way to protect Clay was exactly what she was doing: going after Scarlet.

"How are you going to find your friends in Possibility?" she asked Turtle. "It's a big city. Full of dragons who have irrationally negative feelings about me. And too many wooden buildings too close together. I don't like it. For the record, it's a stupid place."

"You've mentioned that," Turtle said, glancing over his shoulder again. "Can we rest for the night and figure it out in the morning when we get there? My wings are so sore, I swear they're about to fall off. They've never been in this much pain ever."

Peril traced the river below them with her eyes, up to the town in the near distance. It was *so close.*

Then again, why was she hurrying to get somewhere she didn't even want to be at all?

"All right," Peril agreed. "Let's find a spot with fewer trees and more rocks."

The sun was sinking way out beyond the desert when they came down to land near the river, in a spot where giant boulders overlapped one another halfway into the water and small rapids bustled noisily around them.

Peril tried to be careful, but there were too many patches of moss, and she felt a twinge of familiar guilt as some of them curled into blackened ash below her claws. Also, as she settled on a boulder, her tail slipped into a little pool nearby, and immediately boiled the two fish swimming there. They floated to the surface, white bellies turned up to the purpling sky.

"Shoot," Peril said. "I mean . . . hey, look, dinner."

Turtle splashed over through the river, speared one of the fish with a claw, and winced. "Yowch. I don't think I could ever get used to eating hot prey. It's such a weird feeling in my mouth."

"I've never eaten prey any other way," Peril pointed out. "It's always black and crunchy." *A little like the black rocks Queen Scarlet tricked me into eating when I was younger.* The queen had convinced Peril that because of her firescales condition, she needed to eat a certain kind of black rock every day. It could only be found in the mountains, and Scarlet took charge of Peril's supply. *"I'm the one keeping you alive." That's what she always said.*

But it was a lie . . . a trick to keep Peril confined to the Sky Palace and dependent on Queen Scarlet. Even though Peril had always obeyed the queen's every order, Scarlet still never trusted her.

What did she think I would do? Run away? Try to steal the throne? Join the Talons of Peace?

Think for myself?

Peril shook off that thought with a growl.

It wasn't personal, though, she had to remind herself. Queen Scarlet manipulated everyone she came into contact with, not only Peril.

"Well, that's just sad," Turtle said, and after a minute Peril realized he was still talking about how she only ate burnt prey. He rolled his shoulders back and forth, stretching his neck and making agonized faces at his sore muscles. "You should try it the normal way. Here, open your mouth and I'll throw some in." He snared another fish from the river beside his boulder.

"That sounds insane," Peril observed. "What are you talking about?"

"Keep your mouth open and the fish won't touch your scales," he said, placidly ripping the fish into small pieces. "That way it won't get burned, and you can see what it tastes like to most dragons."

Dubiously, Peril stretched her jaws wide open.

A fish head smacked her in the eye.

"YUCK!" she roared, surging up with her wings flared. "Try that again, SeaWing!"

"I'm sorry!" he yelped. "Sorry, sorry, sorry! I missed. Here, let me try again."

She eyed him suspiciously. He looked not so much "deeply repentant," as "trying to hide his giggles."

"Did you do that on purpose?" she demanded.

"No, I swear," he said. "But I don't have very good aim. Not a lot of practice. Give me another chance?"

Growling softly, Peril opened her mouth again.

The next two pieces sailed straight past her head, but the third finally splatted between her teeth, and she snapped her jaws shut around it. It felt like a cold slimy frog had just leaped into her mouth. She chewed for a moment, as long as she could bear it, and then swallowed fast.

"No," she said. "Definitely no. Horrifying amounts of no. That was one hundred percent disgusting."

Turtle laughed. "You're so wrong," he said. "It's awesome. That's how fish *should* be eaten."

"Blergh," Peril said strongly. She hopped to the next boulder, heading for the shore. "I'm going to find something that is the opposite of fish, scorch it, and then coat my tongue with char to get that taste out of my mouth. YUUUCK. You are the worst. I would be so justified in setting you on fire while you're asleep tonight."

"Duly noted," Turtle said serenely. "Did I mention I'll be sleeping at the bottom of the river? You know, if you're looking for me." He grinned at her.

Peril paused on the riverbank, squinting at him. She had been joking, of course. There were a number of excellent reasons not to set Turtle on fire, which outweighed any potential benefits to doing so. But it unsettled her for a moment to realize that by sleeping in the river — even by standing in the river right now — he could foil any plan she *did* make, if she ever needed to burn him up.

Not that I would. Probably. I most likely would never need to. And I wouldn't want to, of course, that, too.

But she'd never run into a situation where someone could stop her like that, apart from Clay.

Maybe I did have an unfair advantage fighting SeaWings in the arena. If I were fighting them in their own part of the world — somewhere they could go underwater to escape, or even drag me underwater with them . . .

She didn't like that train of thought. She didn't like ONE SINGLE THING about it.

"I'll be back in a minute," she snapped.

"I'll be here, apologizing to my woebegone wings," he said.

She stomped off, ignoring the trail of scorched grass she left in her wake as she searched the shoreline for prey. After a few minutes, a hare bolted out of a burrow in front of her, and she was able to catch it and wolf it down.

On her way back, she caught sight of Turtle lying on one of the boulders. The sun was halfway down, casting warm orange light across his dark green scales. And the SeaWing was doing something odd. She paused to stare at him for a moment. It looked as if he was rolling a small river stone across his shoulders.

"What are you doing?" she asked, coming up behind him.

He jumped, looking *fascinatingly* guilty. There was definitely *something* not right about this.

"Nothing," he said. "Just trying to work out the kinks in my back. I've never flown this much before."

"So you've mentioned a few hundred times," Peril said. "Can I see the rock you're using?"

"Oh, this?" he said. "Just a rock I picked up from the river." He held it out casually, the smooth gray-white stone looking like a hawk's egg in his webbed talons.

"Does it really help?" she asked.

"Uh," he said. "A little." He rolled his shoulders again. "Anyway. Woo, I'm tired. I'll see you in the morning!"

He dove into the water and vanished below the surface, taking the rock with him.

Peril sat down on her boulder and flipped her tail over her talons. It was hard to tell in the growing dusk, but she was pretty sure the blurry shape of Turtle was still applying the rock to his scales underwater.

That was weird, she mused. *He could have stayed up here and talked to me for a* little *bit longer. Did he think I was going to steal his rock? Is it some kind of SeaWing secret I shouldn't know — river rocks can heal them or something?*

That sounded pretty implausible, even to someone who had been raised not to know much about other tribes.

Maybe he was simply trying to get away from her. Maybe he'd finally realized, like every other dragon in the world, that she was a terrible dragon to be friends with.

But he'd been laughing with her only a few minutes earlier . . .

Doesn't matter, she thought fiercely. *Whatever it is, that's just fine. He can keep his secrets or stop being friends with me or whatever he wants.*

I can always go back to Clay. My real friend.

You're not that important to me either, SeaWing.

Hmph.

She lay down and closed her eyes, but sleep was a long time coming.

CHAPTER 7

The next morning, Turtle was mostly normal. A little jittery, but it could have been excitement about being so close to finding his winglet again.

His friends — and then he'll probably ditch me, Peril realized. She guessed the others wouldn't be too thrilled about her coming along. Especially that IceWing, if he was still alive and around anywhere.

Well, if she had to find Scarlet on her own, that was probably better anyway.

She sat on the boulder where she'd slept, watching Turtle splash around after his breakfast. He had a small waterproof pouch around his neck, which looked heavier than usual this morning. From the way it thumped against his chest, Peril guessed that he'd put one of the river rocks in there.

His only other accessory was a gold armband with three sparkly black rocks set in it, plus three holes where it seemed as though other rocks should have been. Peril had noticed that he fiddled with it when he was nervous, sticking his claws into the holes and tugging the armband up and down.

"Why are you glaring at me?" Turtle asked.

"I'm not GLARING," Peril snapped. "This is my FACE."

"Your *face* kind of looks like it hates me today," Turtle observed. "Can you remind it that I'm really quite nice?"

Peril concentrated on her expression for a moment, but she could feel her frown only getting deeper. "All right, now I'm glaring at you," she said. "Can we get on with this annoying day already?"

"Are you nervous about going to Possibility?" Turtle said shrewdly. "We won't have to be there long. Maybe no one will even notice you."

"You really have no idea what it's like to be me," Peril said, arching her neck and flaring her wings. The rising sun slammed into her scales, scattering into bright orange reflections in the water below her. "I've never NOT been noticed. That's not an option for me. Imagine my life as the literal opposite of yours."

He didn't answer. Peril squinted at him and realized he was peering at a spot along the muddy shore of the river.

"What?" she demanded. "What's so fascinating?"

"I'm guessing these talonprints aren't yours," he said.

Peril hopped into the river and splashed over to him,

sending up clouds of steam all around her. Turtle didn't flail away in a panic like most dragons would. He moved over quietly so she could see the mud, where a set of prints were clearly embedded, along with the sweep of a tail around them.

Someone had been standing here, then sitting here, very recently. Someone bigger than Peril, facing the river . . . facing the boulder where she'd been sleeping.

"HELLO?" Peril yelled, making Turtle jump. "If you're spying on us, just come out already!"

Turtle rubbed his ears. "So *stealth* isn't your strong suit either, I see."

"Sorry," Peril said unrepentantly. "I know it's your *only* suit. WHOEVER YOU ARE, JUST COME OUT AND SAY WHATEVER YOU HAVE TO SAY!"

There was no response. The leaves on the trees whispered quietly, as if gossiping about the crazy copper dragon shouting at nothingness.

Peril shrugged. "I guess they left. Maybe they just wanted to catch a glimpse of a fire monster. Or maybe they thought I was Scarlet and then realized who I am and fled in terror! That could be it."

"Hmmm," Turtle said, with just a shade too much skepticism in his voice. He twisted around, scanning the trees and sky and river, but there was no sign of anybody.

"I have a plan for Possibility," Peril said. "Let's go." She spread her wings and launched herself into the sky like a burst of flames. The sun had crept over the mountaintops, spilling in golden stripes down the canyons and across the hills. To the west, Peril saw a line of camels plodding across the desert with smaller shapes on their backs and around their heels — scavengers, perhaps.

Turtle flapped wetly up beside her, splattering her with spray from his tail and wings. In the sunlight, his jewel-toned scales looked more like emeralds than ever. "A plan would be good," he said. "Tell me your plan."

"Easy. We'll just dive right into the middle of the market, and then all those dragons will start stampeding around yelling about what a menace I am, and then you shout, 'Moon and Qibli, meet us outside town!' and then we fly away again." Peril nodded with satisfaction. "I think that would work."

Turtle wrinkled his snout at her. "I have a slightly less insane idea," he said. "If you can swim."

"I can do anything," Peril said, tossing her head. "There was a lake by this waterfall near the Sky Palace that I swam in once. I didn't like it, though." It was weird, being surrounded by water. In a way, it was like flying, because she couldn't exactly burn anything while she was underwater. But it was also unsettling. Dragons shouldn't be underwater. *Fire* shouldn't be underwater.

"If we swim into the city, no one will notice you," Turtle said. "We'll be able to scout it out without attracting a lot of attention."

"I don't care about attention," Peril said. "If a dragon wants to stare at me and hate me and think horrible thoughts about all the things they *can't* do to me, then they can go right ahead."

She twisted around to glance back at Turtle. A movement far below them caught her eye, and she angled one wing to look down.

There was a black dragon standing on the boulder where Peril had slept the night before.

He lowered his snout for a moment — studying the moss she'd burned? — and then lifted his head to scan the sky.

Although he was miles away now, Peril felt his eyes snag on her scales like wickedly sharp fishhooks.

He didn't move. He didn't come flying after them.

He just stared, eerie and still, watching her beat more and more distance between them, getting smaller and smaller.

Whoever he was, Peril had a feeling he wasn't done with her yet.

Turtle did a flip in the sky to see what she was looking at. He nearly lost the wind under him as he spotted the dragon.

"I was right!" he cried. "See? He's following us!"

"He's not," Peril pointed out. "Mostly he's just staring at us. It's creepy, but to be fair, if he tried to do that from any closer up, I'd have to stick something sharp and burning into his eyeballs."

"All right," Turtle said. "Thank you for that visual. Do you know any NightWings?"

"Starflight," Peril answered. "And that other fluff-brained one at the school, but it's too big to be either of them."

Turtle flicked his tail nervously and beat his wings faster, keeping up with her easily for the first time since they'd left Jade Mountain. "I did hear a rumor . . ." he started.

"A rumor?" Peril asked. "Or dragons having a conversation you weren't supposed to overhear?"

"Nobody said I couldn't stand in the tunnel outside and listen!" Turtle said defensively. "Anyway, Sunny was telling Tsunami that some NightWing prisoners had escaped from Thorn's stronghold. Maybe it's one of them."

"Why would a NightWing prisoner be interested in us?" Peril asked.

"True. Maybe it's someone working with Scarlet," Turtle said. "Maybe it's her new ally."

Peril swiveled violently around in the sky. *How did I not think of that? What if it's a NightWing animus? Coming after me on Scarlet's orders? Maybe I'm higher on her vengeance list than I thought . . .*

The black dragon was gone.

"Wonderful," she said. "You couldn't have mentioned that a bit sooner? Now all I can do is WORRY about it. I HATE worrying about things."

"It's almost time for us to swim," Turtle said cheerfully. "You can worry about that instead." He canted his wings and swooped down toward the river.

Uneasily, Peril followed him. *Don't think about it. There's nothing I can do about this NightWing right now anyway. I have to wait until he shows his face a bit closer to me, and then I can burn it off, and then everything will be fine.*

She flexed her talons, feeling the warm shift of her fire-scales, and then splashed down right behind Turtle.

The river was cold and extremely wet and full of flappy slippery things. Peril did not like it ONE BIT. The flappy slippery things (she assumed most of them were fish) kept *touching* her and then *not* bursting into flames and that was *so weird.* Even the feeling of water all around her scales, pressing in on her, was extremely unsettling.

She was also not particularly fond of how much faster than her Turtle could suddenly go. He powered forward in huge wingbeats, steering gracefully with the current, while she flopped around snorting water up her snout and generally feeling like a hippo.

A hippo floated past, eyeing her with serene scorn.

Fine. Not like a hippo. Like an ostrich suddenly plunked in the middle of an ocean, how about that.

Far ahead, Turtle swerved majestically around a bend in the river and clambered onto a submerged boulder to wait for her. Peril floundered toward him, finally finding pebbles below her talons and a moment to gasp for breath.

"Couldn't we fly a little closer?" she spat.

"Not if we want you to arrive incognito." Turtle pointed to the increasing number of dragons flying overhead. The wings flashing in the sky were mostly red, orange, or sandy yellow, although Peril spotted shades of brown and blue up there as well. "Don't worry, soon we'll be swimming into Possibility. Hopefully no one will notice your scales underwater, and hopefully we'll be able to spot Moon and Qibli from the river."

He dove back into the river and Peril had no choice but to follow him. The outskirts of Possibility swept up on either side of the riverbank. These were the smaller dwellings of dragons who'd moved to the city recently. Peril swam past a family of SeaWings who splashed in the shallows, blue scales flickering like broken shards of sky. The two dragonets yelped and wrestled while their father watched, smiling in a way that no one had ever, ever smiled at Peril.

A little farther downstream, on the other side of the river, three MudWings near Peril's age were planting a garden. The biggest one pointed to a crooked furrow and thwapped one of her siblings bossily. Her brother flung a carrot at her, and the third sibling giggled until she nearly fell over. It wasn't until the MudWings were behind them that Peril realized the littlest sister had been missing an arm.

She took a closer look at the next set of dragons they passed and spotted another war wound, a scar that ran nearly the length of the SkyWing's tail. But this dragon, too, was smiling, leaning over to show a smaller dragon how to fix a broken doorframe. He must have felt her staring at him, because he turned his head toward the river, but Peril submerged her head and swam faster, and when she surfaced again there was an island between them.

More islands began to dot the river as it widened out and the current slowed, sometimes trailing into wandering streams or muddling about in clumps of tall reeds. Peril and Turtle swam under a bridge packed end-to-end with merchant stalls and dragons calling out to customers. ("The finest rugs in Possibility!" "The *actual* finest rugs in Possibility!" "Roasted crocodile on sale!" "Don't eat that! His crocodile was rotting in the streets yesterday! *We* have seagulls caught in the air this morning!")

The next bridge glowed with bright colors and shook with thumping talons as dragons danced along its length. Peril could feel the music vibrating in the water around her. Beaten silver circles hung from the railings and under the bridge like giant coins.

"A full-moon festival," Turtle said, popping his head out of the water right next to her. "It used to be a SandWing tradition, but they didn't have much time for them during the war. I heard they were coming back."

Peril floated under the bridge, watching the whirling dragons overhead as they clapped their wings and twined their tails together. She would never dance in a crowd like that, wearing bangles of silver moons and singing until her voice cracked. She would never paint huge canvases side by side with other SkyWings and SandWings, dipping their tails into the same buckets of moonlit white and midnight blue paint and laughing as it spattered across their claws and snouts.

She'd been in this town only four months ago, searching for Scarlet, but something was different now. It felt lighter and more open than before. As if the war was starting to melt away . . . as if their world was starting to feel safer under Thorn and Ruby than it ever had been with Burn and Scarlet.

But it's not safe. Not as long as Queen Scarlet is still out there, smoldering with hate.

"Moon should be easy to spot here," Turtle said, his snout half buried in the water so his voice rose through bubbles. "Not a lot of NightWings around."

No NightWings at all that Peril could see. She wondered if they knew about this place, and whether any of them would eventually choose to come here. It wouldn't suit their tribal air of mystery, mingling with so many other dragons like this . . . but on the other talon, it might give them more self-respect than living under a RainWing queen's claws.

She'd never been to the rainforest herself. Clay had strongly discouraged the idea, saying something about how many trees there were and forest fires and blah blah blah. But that was fine; Peril was sure she wouldn't like feeling so hemmed in anyway. It sounded claustrophobic. Plus full of dragons who could sneak up on you with, like, invisibility scales — that sounded absolutely creepy. Not to mention that Queen Glory was far from Peril's biggest fan.

The drums and zithers of the full-moon festival were starting to fade behind them, and Peril could see glimmers of the open bay ahead in the distance. This part of Possibility seemed to have older, bigger, sturdier buildings set around open cobblestoned plazas. The palm trees looked more deliberately spaced, casting strategic patches of shade. Bright yellow trumpet-shaped flowers swarmed along dark green vines that seemed to be tangled everywhere.

"Wait," Turtle said, turning so suddenly that he splashed water up Peril's nose. She backpedaled against the current, scowling at him.

"What?" she said. "Can we give up now? We could just fly over the town — it'll be easier to spot a black dragon from up there anyhow. It's not like anyone is going to come up and try to fight me."

"I thought I saw Qibli," Turtle said. He spread his wings to float in a circle and craned his neck, peering at the dragons along the waterfront. "Those SandWings over there, arguing with the red SkyWing — doesn't one of them look like Qibli?"

Peril realized that she didn't have the faintest idea what Qibli looked like. Had she ever met him before? All SandWings looked pretty much the same to her, apart from Sunny, of course, who had oddly colored scales and a perpetually cheerful expression that was just asking to be clawed off. "Uh — sure?"

"Let's go see." Turtle charged out of the river before Peril could argue. His emerald green tail left a slick wet path on the cobblestones behind him.

She scanned the nearby dragons, but they were all focused on their own business; no one was watching the river. And now she could see the dragons Turtle was aiming for. The red SkyWing stood with his wings folded back and his head cocked arrogantly at the two burly SandWings in front of him, one of whom was lashing her menacing tail. Both SandWings were wearing medallions around their necks stamped with the image of a large bird. Arranged on the stones around their talons were several odd-looking brownish-greenish-pink spheres studded with little spikes.

Peril slithered out of the water and hurried after Turtle, keeping her head low and her wings tucked in close.

"You said thirty!" she heard the bigger SandWing yell. "That was the agreement!"

"You are welcome to come to the mountains and try harvesting these yourself," spat the SkyWing. "It is much more difficult than your paltry pouch of gold would cover."

"Let's just take them," the male SandWing growled.

"He won't be pleased and you know it," his partner snapped.

Turtle paused several feet away from them and turned back to Peril, shaking his head. *Not Qibli.* She stopped, too, in the most empty patch of stone she could find. From here, the plaza became cluttered with wares spread on carpets, flowers growing out of window boxes, and dragons blithely trampling around everywhere without worrying at all about whose scales they might blunder into. Danger tingled just beyond Peril's reach; she could sense all the terrible things that might happen if she stepped any farther into the town.

She needed to get back to the river, where she wouldn't be such a threat.

She glanced around and began to cautiously turn, keeping her tail curled safely in.

And then one of the SandWings muttered something furious and kicked one of the spheres.

Oh, it's a cactus, Peril realized, spotting the roots as it bounced across the stones toward her. *I've seen those in the mountains, I think.*

She glanced up, and the last thing Peril saw was Turtle's green eyes widening as the sphere rolled up to her talons — brushed against her scales — and exploded in an enormous fireball.

CHAPTER 8

Peril came to because her body decided not to drown. She surged up out of the water where the explosion had thrown her, coughing and sputtering, into a cloud of thick black smoke that was not particularly fun to breathe either.

Her eyes were stinging and everything was blurry and muffled, but she could see there were dragons yelling and screaming all along the bank and more flapping in from the rooftops. At least three dragons were rolling in the river with scorch marks on their scales. Small fires flickered in the smoke all across the courtyard.

She wasn't burned — her scales couldn't burn — but there were incredibly sharp blossoms of pain spiking all up and down her body. WHAT WAS THIS. WHY DID IT HURT SO MUCH. WHO COULD SHE SET ON FIRE TO MAKE IT STOP.

She roared her agony as loud as she could, but it made barely a scratch in the jangling chaos all around.

A dragon suddenly came galloping into the river beside her and she jumped back, hissing at him, before she recognized Turtle.

"You," he said, shaking his head, "are without question the *least* stealthy dragon in all of Pyrrhia."

"That wasn't my fault," she snarled, writhing in pain. Nothing had ever managed to hurt her like this. There were tiny teeth eating under her scales! "EVERYTHING HURTS AND I HATE THE WORLD."

"Let's find a safer place to be before someone sees you and connects the dots," Turtle said. She realized that trickles of blood were running down his shoulders and along his tail. He waded into the water until it covered everything but his head and began swimming upstream, back toward the full-moon festival bridge.

It was agony to move, but she did, flailing after him and hoping the smoke would hide her shining copper scales.

Turtle finally coasted to a stop in clearer air, on the muddy bank of one of the small islands, not far from where the festival music was still going on. He pulled himself half onto the shore, wincing, and Peril crawled up into the mud as far away from him as she could. The reeds and shrubs below her curled into a dark scorched mess, but she was in too much pain to worry about it. She wondered if this was what being on fire felt like to other dragons.

"*Why*," she growled. "What is HAPPENING."

"It was a dragonflame cactus," Turtle said. He twisted and started to pry at something stuck under his left wing in a small pool of blood. "Like the one that exploded in the history cave at school. I have no idea why anyone would want to buy one now that the war is over."

They didn't want to buy just one, Peril remembered. *They wanted to buy thirty*. Whatever their reason was, she thought perhaps burning out their eyeballs would make her feel better.

Turtle extracted the object from his scales and held it out for her to see. "It's like a little ball of thorns," he said. "The dragonflame cactus seedpod. You have about a hundred of them stuck all over you, since it exploded right at your feet. But I don't know what to do — I can't pull them out of your scales without getting burned — but we can't leave them — oh . . ." He trailed off, staring at her.

"What?" Peril demanded. She was starting to feel a little better, maybe, now that she was out of the water.

"They're burning up," Turtle explained. "Your scales are burning the seedpods away."

Peril held out one front leg and saw a ball of thorns embedded between her claws, right before it caught fire and shriveled into black ash.

"That's right," she said. "DIE, you little monster plants.

May your roots always be thirsty and your seeds all meet a fiery death until you're extinct forever! I HATE you!"

"Yowch," Turtle said. "You don't ever have mild feelings, do you?"

Peril wasn't sure what a "mild" feeling would feel like. She turned to blink downriver at the pillar of black smoke rising from the distant courtyard.

"Was, um . . . did you see if the explosion . . . uh . . ." Peril trailed off.

"I don't think anyone was killed," Turtle said. "It looked like your body blocked the worst of the fire and caught most of the seedpods. I saw other dragons injured, but nobody like —"

"Nobody like Carnelian," Peril finished. She tried to hide the relief in her voice. Although Clay would forgive her for an accident, surely? Even if someone had died? It wouldn't *really* be her fault, except in the sense that everything was her fault because she was a walking menace to the entire universe.

"Anyway," Peril said indignantly, "what kind of idiot spreads a bunch of flammable cacti all over the street? Anyone could have set one of those off by accident!"

"Not a SeaWing," Turtle said thoughtfully. "Or an IceWing. Oh, hey, now we know one more thing that *can't* kill you."

. "They shouldn't be allowed to sell things like that to just anyone," Peril went on, ignoring him. She twitched her tail around to check for any more thorns, but they all seemed to be gone. "Would they sell a *sword* to any dragon who came along?"

"Um," Turtle said. "Yes?" His smile fell off his face as he winced again. Another ball of thorns was dripping blood down his tail, but he couldn't twist far enough to reach it.

"I could set it on fire," Peril offered, spreading her claws. "But it might burn you a little bit. I don't know if that would be worse."

Turtle thought for a moment, then shuffled a step toward her. "Yes. Do it. If I jump straight into the river after, I'll be fine."

Peril hadn't actually expected him to say yes. Nobody ever let her help with anything. Even Clay usually got sort of flappy and nervous whenever she offered.

She folded her wings back and reached forward tentatively with one claw. Turtle closed his eyes, frozen in place.

Peril's claw lightly brushed the thorny seedpod, and it burst into flames. Immediately she saw a dark scorched patch start to spread where the thorns touched Turtle's scales, but she only caught a glimpse of it before Turtle dove into the water and swam to the bottom.

She paced along the bank, trying to squint at him through the shifting reflections. He was a huddled green lump at the bottom of the river for way too long — it made her own lungs ache to wait for him. But he was clearly fine, definitely moving, and fiddling with something that flashed white-gray.

Weird.

Finally he surfaced, spraying water out of his nose and looking extremely pleased with himself. Peril's eyes went straight to the spot where she'd burned him . . . but there was no scorch mark there anymore. His scales looked whole and unblemished all over, as if neither fire nor thorns had ever wounded him. She couldn't even figure out where the seedpods had been.

"How did you do *that*?" she demanded. "Water doesn't heal SeaWings that quickly."

"It wasn't that bad," Turtle said with a shrug. "I'm fine. Don't worry."

"I'm not *worried*, I'm *deeply suspicious*," Peril clarified. "That's not normal scale behavior right there."

"Turtle?"

They both jumped at the voice that came from the sky. Peril realized she'd been watching Turtle so closely she hadn't kept an eye out for approaching danger — or anyone who might realize she'd set off the cactus. *Genius, Peril. If there is an animus NightWing stalking you, you're making it pretty easy for him.*

But the dragon above them was a SandWing, and Turtle gave a cry of delight when he saw him.

"Qibli!" Turtle leaped into the air and nearly bowled him out of the sky. They swooped around each other for a moment, doing cheerful flips in the air and thumping one another's wings, which appeared to be some kind of code for "happy to see you." A moment later, a small NightWing came soaring over from the direction of the explosion and Turtle made more dopey delighted noises at her.

I guess we found his friends. Peril flicked her tail and accidentally splashed herself in the face. *Probably thanks to me, by the way. I bet they came to check out the fire. I wonder if Turtle will realize that.*

She stood up and paced in a circle in the mud. All the places she'd been stabbed with thorns still hurt, but at least the seedpods were gone. Maybe she should fly away before Turtle came down with his judgmental friends. Maybe she didn't need anyone else to look for Scarlet anyhow.

But it was too late; green and black and yellow wings were descending toward the island, along with three dragon faces that ranged from friendly through wary and straight on to hostile.

Which is just fine, Peril thought, meeting Qibli's eyes with all the fire she could put into hers. *I am prepared to dislike you, too. Who cares what you think? Are YOU the most dangerous dragon in Pyrrhia, NO, I THINK NOT.*

"Peril, this is Moon and Qibli," said Turtle, beaming all over his stupid round face as if this should be the most delightful thing that had ever happened to any of them.

She couldn't remember noticing either of these dragons before. They looked completely ordinary, not like anyone worth crossing an entire continent to find. Not like dragons who were so much more awesome to be friends with than her.

The NightWing had a glittering silver scale at the corners of each eye, like teardrops, and little furrows in her forehead as though she had a perpetual headache. Now that everyone knew NightWings didn't have powers after all, Peril was sure Moon would be an easy opponent to take down in the arena. Hypothetically, if there still had been an arena, of course.

The SandWing didn't look like much of a threat either, apart from that venomous tail. Peril had been in plenty of fights where her first move was grabbing a SandWing's tail to burn off the barb at the end. As long as Scarlet didn't need her to drag out the fight, most SandWings only took a few minutes to defeat. No doubt this one was pretty dim and cor-respondingly slow.

"You're wrong about that," Moon said.

Peril shifted her gaze to the black dragon, who was study-ing Peril intently. "What?" Peril asked.

"Qibli is probably one of the smartest dragons in Pyrrhia," Moon answered. "I bet he's already figured out five different ways to defeat you right here if he needed to."

Qibli cocked his head and gave Moon a delighted side-ways smile. "Only three so far," he said. "But thanks."

Peril blinked at Moon, feeling like little dragonflame cacti were going off inside her head. "Did you — but —"

"Yes," Moon said. "I'm a mind reader. So you should *prob-ably* stop thinking about how exactly you would kill us if you needed to."

"Was she really?" Turtle said, sounding perfectly astonished, as if that wasn't the first thing *most* dragons thought about when they met dragons outside their own tribes.

(Wasn't it?)

Peril whipped her head around to glare at Turtle. "You brought me to meet a mind reader?" she said. "And you didn't think that might be worth *mentioning* sometime before now?"

Was this a test? Maybe this was his plan all along . . . maybe he never trusted me, like Scarlet never trusted me, and he wanted to see what Moon would find in my head . . .

Turtle shrugged. "It's Moon's secret. It's up to her who she tells."

"I'm not entirely sure why Scarlet's Dancing Monkey of Fiery Doom gets to be on that list, frankly," said Qibli.

"And remind me, you're Thorn's Dancing Monkey of what, exactly?" Peril demanded. "At least I was *useful* to *my* queen."

"I told her," Moon interjected, opening one wing pointedly between them before Qibli could lunge at Peril, "because it's the right thing to do, and because there's no way to give her any skyfire, and also because I am hoping that if she knows I'm listening, she'll try to have less disturbing thoughts."

That sounded complicated. Peril wrinkled her snout. *How am I supposed to change my thoughts? They just appear in my head. I've never had to worry about them DISTURBING anyone before.*

"Maybe you should stop listening instead," Peril said.

Moon shook her head. "It doesn't work that way. But don't worry about it too much . . . your thoughts are actually really hard to hear. Mostly all I get from your mind is heat and flames and —" She broke off, twitching her wings back awkwardly for a moment. "Anyway, it's not as clear as most minds. You're mostly safe from me."

"Tremendously comforting," Peril said. She tried to fill up her head with more fire, hoping to burn out anything she didn't want Moon to see, although really that was either everything or nothing. Whatever Moon already thought of her, from whatever scraps of thoughts she'd heard, none of the rest would make any difference — either she could stand all of Peril just the way she was, or she'd hate her for a small piece of her as much as for all the rest of it.

Now she was giving herself a headache.

"Is Kinkajou all right?" Turtle asked. "Where is she?"

"And your hostile ice dragon?" Peril added.

"Winter's gone back to the Ice Kingdom," Moon said. She glanced at Qibli. "Qibli thinks he's coming back, but I'm not so sure. Kinkajou is . . . well, she's recovering, we think, but she still hasn't woken up." She blinked several times rapidly. "She would be *so* excited to see you here," she said to Turtle with a sad smile.

"We were attacked by a dragon who's working with Scarlet," Qibli said. He squinted at Peril, then turned to Moon. "What did she think about that? Can you tell if she's working for Scarlet, too?"

"No, I don't think she is," said Moon, ". . . buuuut now she's gone back to fantasizing about ways to kill you."

"Because that was RUDE," Peril flared. "Poking around inside my brain to find the answer to a question I've already answered over and over. You can go stuff a mountain goat up your nose, SandWing! Horns first! I'm looking for Scarlet to *stop* her, not help her. Why are there so many stupid dragons who can't see that?"

"Well," Qibli said, "you *did* help her escape from Burn's stronghold not *that* long ago."

"That —" Peril sputtered. "That was just — that — but Burn was the bad guy then! I couldn't leave my queen trapped in that place. Nobody would!"

"Your queen?" Qibli challenged. "Isn't Ruby your queen now?"

Peril drew herself up, glaring at him, knowing that Moon must be hearing all her fears about Ruby scattering about inside her head. "I don't have to explain myself to you, sand snorter. We are only here to find out what you know about where Scarlet is." She turned her fierce gaze on Moon and the NightWing flinched. "Then I'll take my *disturbing* thoughts right out of your life forever. Is the plan."

"It's true, we have to find her," Turtle explained. "She attacked Jade Academy!" Moon blinked and Qibli's tail arched reflexively, his talons digging into the mud.

"She did *not*," Peril said, rolling her eyes at him. "She flew by, threw a decapitated head at us, and flew away again.

That wasn't an *attack*. That was more like a declaration of war. If she ever decides to really attack you, you'll know."

"A decapitated head?" Moon echoed with alarm. "Sunny said Scarlet was there making threats . . . but she didn't mention a head."

"Was it our fault?" Qibli asked immediately. "She must be furious about us escaping with Hailstorm. What if we enraged her into coming out of hiding?"

"That seems extremely likely," Peril said. "I imagine just meeting you would enrage Queen Scarlet to the point of wanting to kill several dragons."

"Ha ha!" Turtle said, as though Peril were kidding, which she clearly was not. "So where did you encounter Scarlet?"

"In a part of the mountains not far from here," Moon said. "But I'm sure she wouldn't still be there. I don't see how we can help you . . . the only way we found her before was because she was using the dreamvisitor and left clues."

Peril hated that dreamvisitor. Scarlet showed up in her dreams ALL THE TIME, and half the time Peril wasn't even sure if she was real. Whether she was or not, there was always yelling and guilt and ominous remarks about Clay's future.

"I knew they wouldn't be helpful," she said to Turtle.

"Well," Turtle said uncertainly, "maybe if you show us on a map where she was, we can at least start searching from there."

Qibli looked up at the sky, where the sun was meandering toward the midpoint. "Sure, but right now we should get back to the clinic. The dragons from Glory are supposed to arrive soon."

Peril wondered if he was changing the subject because he didn't trust her. *Consider the feeling mutual, SandWing,* she thought, eyeing him narrowly.

"The clinic? Where Kinkajou is?" Turtle's face brightened hopefully, then fell as he turned toward Peril. "But Peril can't go into the city."

She spread her gold-veined wings to indicate *Remember? Deadly firescales over here?* but she accidentally hit a branch overhead, which burst into flames.

Qibli promptly smacked his tail in the river, sending up a wave that cascaded over the branch *and* Peril, soaking her and putting the fire out.

Peril regarded him coldly, water dripping from her snout.

"Don't feel bad," Moon said to Turtle. "Kinkajou wouldn't know you were there anyway."

Turtle's wings drooped, and Peril had a sudden very strong feeling that there was a right thing to say here. It was written in the slump of his shoulders and the way he poked one claw gloomily at the mud puddle beside him.

Something reassuring about Kinkajou?

No . . . something else. Something she didn't want to say, but she saw that she kind of had to, and the others were even leaving an odd moment of quiet in the conversation, waiting for her to say it.

"You should go," she said, forcing it out past the growl in her throat. "I'll just . . . wait for you . . . out here . . . somewhere."

"Really?" Turtle said with an enormous smile. "You don't mind? We'll be back soon."

I bet. After you've all talked in secret about me and what you're going to do next and whether to fly off without me.

"Sure," Peril said, then wondered if that sounded sarcastic, and tried again: *"Suuure."* OK, that one sounded worse. "I mean, yes. Fine. I want to go hunt in the desert anyway."

"There's a big sandstone arch west of the city, set up high so you can see practically the whole Kingdom of Sand," Moon said. "That's where Qibli and I have been going to wait for Winter, whenever we're not with Kinkajou or in the library. Let's meet back there."

"Winter still has two more days," Qibli said quietly. "We told him we'd wait a week."

"He's not coming," Moon said. "I've seen inside his mind, Qibli. He's so loyal to his family and his tribe . . . I don't think anything will change that."

Qibli made a face that Peril couldn't figure out. "Moon, sometimes you're so busy listening to what dragons are thinking, you miss the things they're actually *doing*. Which can tell you a lot more about what they're really like."

"That . . . makes no sense," she said.

"Should I bring Kinkajou something?" Turtle said, hopping from one foot to the other in a very un-Turtle-like way. Peril had never seen him expend even an iota more energy than necessary for whatever he was doing. "Flowers? A fish? No, she doesn't like fish. Um. Kumquats?"

He likes Moon and Qibli, Peril guessed, *but he's really here for Kinkajou.*

Why did he even want to travel with me in the first place? He could have come here without me. Did he think I'd be useful protection along the way? He didn't need to pretend to be friends with me. Boring green puddle dragon! Hrrmph.

Peril caught Moon's eyes on her and didn't like whatever mysterious emotion was going on in them — sympathy? Pity? Bewilderment? Whatever she was getting from Peril's brain, Qibli was right — it didn't mean Moon knew anything about her, really.

Peril sat down and started examining her claws as if she found all these dragons exceedingly boring. This was another trick she'd learned from watching Scarlet, although she had a feeling she wasn't conveying quite the right amount of disdain in the tilt of her wings.

"You don't need anything," Qibli said to Turtle. "Just having you there would be enough for her. Maybe she'll be able to hear your voice."

"See you soon, Peril!" Turtle said enthusiastically.

"Yeah, maybe," Peril said to the empty air, drowned out by the flapping of their wings as all three of them took off and headed into the city.

She waited a minute, to be sure they wouldn't turn around, and then she lifted her head to watch the glowing green shape of her supposed friend flying away from her.

CHAPTER 9

Peril didn't quite realize that she was still in pain from the thorn balls until she was up in the air again, flying with muscles that protested with tiny sparks of agony. She gritted her teeth, determined to ignore it until it went away.

She spent the rest of the morning flying out into the desert, chasing down a desert fox (who escaped into a hole and was kind of too cute to eat anyway), and then catching a large white bird in midair and eating that instead. She also set fire to a tall cactus because it was giving her a superior look and she felt like it. One advantage of a desert: she didn't have to worry about forest fires or accidentally scorching a field of SkyWing crops or whatever other reasons the queen had always had for keeping her in the palace.

THE queen. I do still think of her that way. Qibli's words kept going around in her head, which was VERY annoying and made the next cactus over look like tempting kindling as well.

"Isn't Ruby your queen now?" Well . . . yes, technically, but how could you swear loyalty to a queen who didn't even want you in her kingdom?

How could anyone *feel* loyal to a queen who clearly just wanted you dead?

Peril swerved to fly back toward Possibility and saw a huddle of camels a short ways off, to the south. Maybe a camel would make her feel better.

But as she came closer, she saw that the camels were tied to a palm tree and surrounded by bustling scavengers — at least ten of them, setting up tents and scooping water from a small oasis pond.

They all went gratifyingly still when she shot overhead. She studied their upturned faces, which looked like they were mostly eyes. Terrified eyes. She'd never seen such dopey prey; what were they doing out in the open desert, where it would be so easy to catch and eat them?

She'd never eaten a scavenger before. Queen Scarlet always saved them either to fight in the arena or be served at special banquets, which Peril was never invited to, because blah blah setting the guests on fire would be unhospitable blah blah.

She circled around again, trying to decide how hungry she was. As she did, she spotted one scavenger sitting apart from the others, a little ways up the nearest dune. This one wasn't looking up at Peril. Its shoulders were slumped and its head was buried in its little brown arms, so all Peril could see was a thicket of dark fur on top of its head, a sand-colored cloth wrapped around it, and two little brown feet sticking out.

It looked . . . sad.

That's hilarious, Peril thought. *Do camels get sad? Do mountain goats mope? Does a hawk ever have a day where it feels like none of the other hawks want to be friends with it?*

Maybe I should burn up the other scavengers and see if that makes this one feel better.

She thought about it for a moment, but there was something about the curve of the scavenger's back that was almost too achingly familiar, and in the end Peril turned around and flew away, leaving the scavengers and camels to deal with their own problems.

The sandstone arch was easy to find, high on a butte to the west of Possibility, looping out of the ground and back into it in a shape like a RainWing tail. Peril flew through the hole of the archway, feeling her wing tips brush the stone on either side, and then spiraled around to land on top of it.

The desert spread out before her, vast and endless in the hot afternoon sun. When she turned around she could see the whole town of Possibility — the taller structures clustered around the river delta and the trail of smaller ones leading away along the river. From here, the dragons winding through the streets looked no bigger than scavengers, and sometimes it was even hard to tell what color their scales were.

Beyond Possibility, across the eastern horizon, cut the jagged tooth shapes of the Claws of the Clouds Mountains. Scarlet was in there somewhere, Peril was sure of it. The queen wasn't the kind of dragon to let herself be uncomfortable somewhere weird like the rainforest or the mud swamps. She knew the Sky Kingdom perhaps better than anyone, and she must have found somewhere she didn't mind hiding.

A flicker of movement caught Peril's eye, and she swiveled her head to see a dragon winging his way toward her from the edge of Possibility. He was a big golden-orange SkyWing — not anyone she recognized, although it did seem as though he was flying directly toward her.

Maybe he recognized me from all the way down there. Maybe he's coming to yell at me about how I should leave his precious flammable town alone. Is he the one with the basket of snails from last time? Or perhaps I flambéed one of his relatives and he's still grumpy about it.

She flexed her talons. *Well, if he'd like a fight, I'm certainly in the mood for it.*

Clay flashed into her head, wearing his disappointed face. Which was frustrating, because it both made her miss him and also made her want to yell at him that she hadn't killed anybody *yet*, and couldn't he appreciate *that* instead of anticipating her next bad thing?

And then she felt silly, because she was busy getting mad at him for an imaginary conversation, when really she just wished he was there to nudge her wings and tell her what to do next.

The SkyWing was definitely aiming for the arch and looking at her, but when he was only a few wingbeats away he suddenly jerked back with an expression Peril had seen many times before — that wonderful fear/hatred combination that just the sight of her face seemed to magically induce.

Except this time it wasn't for her. He wasn't looking at her anymore; he was looking beyond her. And whatever he saw made him wheel around abruptly and hightail it back to Possibility as fast as he could fly.

Peril turned and scanned the desert sky.

Two more dragons were flying her way. This time it was an IceWing and a big NightWing, coming from the northwest.

Another NightWing, out here?

Could it be one of the ones who escaped from Thorn's prison?

Or Scarlet's ally?

The sunlight sparked and danced across the IceWing's silver scales like a hundred little moons on fire. Peril curled her tail around her talons and watched him with narrow eyes.

She vaguely remembered the IceWings who'd yelled at her in the big entrance hall at Jade Academy, but she doubted she'd be able to pick Winter or his sister out from a crowd of white dragons. Keeping faces in her head wasn't a particular skill of hers. She always forgot to concentrate on storing their features, usually because she was sizing them up as a potential combatant instead.

Mostly she'd never had to remember the dragons she met anyway, since she'd killed almost all the ones who got close enough to be faces in the first place.

She definitely saw the moment when the ice dragon recognized *her*, though. He immediately altered his flight path to hurtle in her direction. And his face wasn't exactly throwing her an enthusiastic full-moon festival.

"What are *you* doing here?" he yelled down at Peril, circling over her head. The NightWing stayed back, beating her wings to hover in place.

"What do you care?" Peril shouted. It made her instantly grumpy to see how he stayed up in the air, forcing her to look up at him as he flew around and around. That was basic dragon etiquette that even Peril knew: if you want to talk to someone on the ground, you land and look them in the eye.

"Did Scarlet send you?" he called.

"Did she send *you*?" she snapped back. "Last I heard, it was *your* sister who was working for her, not me."

That went in, sharp as a SandWing barb. Winter flinched and frowned even harder. "I'm not going to let you hurt my friends, if that's what you're here for."

"That's funny," Peril said. "I mean, the part where you think you could stop me."

Even as she said it, she knew Clay would think it was exactly the wrong thing to say. She knew she was provoking the IceWing on purpose, because she was already having a bad day and he was making it worse, and she knew she should stop and explain everything and tell him where his friends were, but by all the moons, if he couldn't even handle landing to have a civil conversation, then WHY SHOULD SHE DO ALL THE WORK of keeping things polite? SERIOUSLY.

Still, she could probably have guessed what would happen next.

Winter whirled with a roar and shot a blast of frostbreath at one of her wings. As she'd learned over many arena battles with IceWings, this did essentially nothing except make the spot feel numb for a few minutes while her firescales combated the ice.

But it was still *rude* and she didn't *like it*.

She flung herself into the air and blasted fire right back at him. Clay's voice in her head made her aim to his left so she wouldn't actually hurt him . . . but surely it was all right to scare him a little bit.

He shot out of the way, no doubt congratulating himself on moving so quickly rather than realizing she'd deliberately spared him. With a deft flip of his tail, the IceWing dodged below her and then swung up suddenly to frost-breath her back legs before looping away again.

"That doesn't do anything to me, you one-trick dragon," she cried. "How about some claw-to-claw combat, or are you too much of a coward for that?"

Whether or not he was a coward, he was *fast*. He swept around her in dizzying spirals, flashing headaches straight into her skull with every sun-reflecting spin. She lashed out with her front claws, half sure she wouldn't catch him, and half starting not to care if she did because this dragon was SERIOUSLY ASKING FOR IT.

Fighting in the air was hard! How did dragons focus on staying aloft and attacking and defending all at the same time? She'd never practiced against an opponent in the sky. Her wings felt all clumsy and in the way.

Why didn't Scarlet let me learn to fight properly, if this is how dragons normally do it? Why did she only pit me against prisoners with their wings bound?

For the first time in her life, Peril began to wonder if maybe she *wasn't* actually the most dangerous dragon in Pyrrhia.

But I am! I am! I just have to touch him and he's dead!

Wait.

That would be BAD.

That would be very, very bad, Peril suddenly remembered. This was one of Clay's Jade Mountain students. He was Turtle's friend. Even though he technically attacked her first, she still *knew* how much trouble she'd be in if she hurt him.

"Stop!" she yelled. "Don't make me kill you!"

Nope, that wasn't the right thing to say either.

She tucked in her wings abruptly and dove toward the arch, trying to put a safe distance between her and Winter.

But at that exact moment, he did another flip to swoop below her again.

And the two dragons collided in midair.

Fire and ice, copper and silver . . . Winter and certain death.

CHAPTER 10

At first, all Peril felt was cold limbs, cold scales, cold wings slamming into hers.

The shock knocked the breath out of her for a moment, and they tangled in startled freefall.

And then Winter started screaming, and Peril shoved him away, and he plummeted toward the ground with smoke already rising from his scales, falling as hard and fast as Peril's heart.

Three moons, what have I done?

"Oh my," said the NightWing in the air above them. Peril had forgotten about her. "Firescales! I haven't seen that in a long time."

"Get help!" Peril yelled. She plunged after Winter, who missed the arch and tumbled to the hard rock below it. At the last minute he managed to spread his wings so it wasn't a crash landing, but as he did Peril saw the ropes of black burns smeared across them. He was burning, burning up everywhere she'd accidentally touched him.

He landed heavily and collapsed, writhing in pain.

"I'm sorry!" Peril cried, landing beside him. "I'm sorry, I'm sorry! I was trying to get away! I didn't mean to burn you, I really didn't! I'm here to help your friends stop Scarlet! Stop dying and listen to me!"

He's going to die. Winter is going to die and Clay is never going to speak to me again. I'm going to be alone forever.

She took a hopeless step toward him, but there was nothing she could do — touching him would only make it worse. Not that it could get worse. Except he'd die faster, and maybe that would be a mercy.

Look at him. I am as bad as everyone thinks I am. I'm the one who did this, me and my monstrous claws.

Peril had never cried; she wasn't sure if she could. But she had felt vast emptiness like this before, opening up inside her . . . when Osprey died, when she had to leave Clay the first time, when she found out her mother was dead, and worst of all, when she saw the dragonbite viper sink its fangs into Clay's leg and she thought he would die and she would lose him and the world would not be worth living in anymore.

This emptiness, though, had freezing winds shrieking through the darkness — shrieking, *"This is your fault, your fault, your fault . . . you deserve to be the most hated dragon in Pyrrhia . . . your fault, your fault . . ."*

"Moon," Winter gasped. "Tell Moon —" He closed his eyes, folding into himself.

"Winter!" a voice shouted from the sky. *"Winter!"*

Of course they were here, just in time to see what Peril had done — to witness her monstrosity. She jumped back out of the way as Moon, Qibli, and Turtle thudded down and surged into a crowd around Winter.

"Winter," Moon cried again, grabbing his front talons in hers. "Oh no, oh no, oh no —"

"It was an accident!" Peril said. "I didn't mean to burn him! I didn't!"

"What are our options?" Qibli said frantically. "I know — Winter, frostbreath your scales! That should numb the injuries long enough to get him to the river. Isn't there a cactus sap that heals burns? Winter, come on, don't pass out. We can fix this!"

The silver dragon lay limply on the rocks in front of them, shuddering in agony. He didn't respond to either Moon or Qibli. Peril couldn't bear to look at him — at the black scorch marks imprinted all over his snow-white scales. That had to be too many burns to survive. He was probably going into shock, if he hadn't already.

She couldn't look at Turtle either. He was clutching his head and pacing around Winter's tail, and she knew if she met his eyes she'd see how much he must hate her now.

"What can we do?" Qibli asked Moon, and when she didn't answer because she was crying too hard, he whirled on Peril. "*What can we do?*"

"I don't know!" Peril cried. "I'm the problem, not the solution!"

"Use this," Turtle said, scrabbling in the pouch around his neck. His voice sounded weird, like it was being mangled as it came out of his throat, and his expression was closer to terror than anger, now that Peril could see it. He yanked the grayish-white river rock from the pouch and held it out. Nothing could have looked more ordinary or useless.

"What?" Qibli said, blinking back tears.

"A rock isn't going to . . ." Peril started, but she trailed off as Turtle pushed Qibli aside and placed the rock on top of one of Winter's burns.

Winter let out a yelp of pain at the sudden contact, and Moon reached toward Turtle's talons — then stopped.

Below the rock, the burn looked as if it was evaporating.

The blackness disappeared, and the scales smoothed over, silver and untouched again.

Turtle moved the rock, sliding it gently over the burns all along Winter's torso and wings. It looked as though he was sweeping snow along behind it; every injury disappeared, every wound knitted itself back together and vanished.

The IceWing's breathing became slower and less ragged. He opened his eyes and watched the progress of the rock, his face a mask of confusion and awe.

Within a few moments, Winter was completely healed.

Everyone stared at Turtle, who very much looked as though he wanted a deep ocean chasm to hide in. He stepped back, awkwardly twisting the rock in his talons as though it was a strange growth that had just appeared. "Did I get all of it?" he asked.

"What —" Moon said. She shook her head and crouched beside Winter, gently running one talon over a patch of smooth scales on his torso. "Turtle, what . . . ?" Her voice faded away, swallowed by the disbelief swooping across her face.

Winter sat up, holding out his talons with an awed expression. His wings cautiously expanded to their full width, then closed again. The burns were really gone.

"Turtle," Qibli said carefully. "Why do you have a magic healing rock? No, wait . . . HOW do you have a magic healing rock?"

Peril couldn't put her thoughts in order. She couldn't wrap her brain around Winter surviving what she'd done. She couldn't even feel relieved yet; it was too immense and strange and impossible. There wasn't any room in her head for all her new questions about Turtle. She pulled her wings in as close as possible, watching Winter's perfectly unharmed scales shift and half expecting him to suddenly collapse into a pile of ashes anyway.

"It's an animus-touched object," Moon said to Turtle. "Where did you get — OH." Her eyes suddenly went as wide as the moons she was named after.

Qibli got it a second later. "You didn't find it somewhere," he said, sounding awestruck. "You *made* it! *You're* an animus dragon!"

"That's your secret," Moon breathed. She had an expression like someone who'd just managed to finally alphabetize a million scrolls exactly right. "An animus."

That's why he thinks he can handle Queen Scarlet, Peril realized.

"Oooorg," Turtle said, shivering his wings. "I've never heard anyone say that out loud before. Nobody else knows. Actually, can we not talk about it? It's really not a big deal."

"NOT A —" Winter suddenly chimed in, then cut himself off with a growl, lashing his tail.

"You could have told me," Peril said to Turtle. Wasn't that what friends did? He hadn't told her about Moon's power because it was "her secret," but he could have told her *this.*

"I was thinking about it," Turtle said to Peril. "I mean, so we're not so different, you and I. Right?"

Well, I never had the option of hiding my "gift," Peril thought. *That's a pretty big difference.*

"Would anyone else like to make a dramatic confession?" Qibli asked. "Who else is hiding magic powers? Winter, anything we should know? A secret IceWing ability to kill dragons with a sneer?"

"No. Trust me, I'm nothing special," Winter growled.

"Same here." Qibli glanced around at Moon, Peril, and Turtle. "At least that makes two of us."

"When did you make this rock?" Moon asked Turtle. "Are you all right? How much have you used your power so far?" She rubbed her forehead, her wings flickering like moths around a candle.

"Don't worry, my soul is fine," Turtle said, waving at the air. "I haven't enchanted very many things. I mean, I didn't want anyone to notice I can do this, obviously."

"But why?" Winter exploded. "Why would you hide your power? You could have served your tribe during the war! Your queen needed you! You could have won the war easily, with a gift like that!"

"Well," Turtle said, shying away from him. "Um. Exactly?"

"Wait, so it would be all right with you," Peril said suddenly to Winter, "for his queen to use *him* as a weapon, but it was the most unforgivable crime in history for my queen to use *me* as one?"

An awkward silence dropped over the group, like a dragonflame cactus full of guilt-suspicion-distrust-judgment-superiority instead of thorn seeds. Nobody would meet Peril's eyes, not even Turtle.

"I get it," Moon said finally to Turtle. "You should be the one who decides what to do with your abilities, not your queen or anyone else."

Now she glanced at Peril quickly, almost as if she were throwing out a tail for Peril to grab.

Me? Peril thought. *Did she mean that for me, too? I never get to decide anything. If I did, I'd probably mess up and nearly kill or really kill someone else.*

"Would that rock work on Kinkajou?" Qibli asked. "Could we heal her, too?"

Turtle squirmed. "We could try," he said. "But I'm afraid I enchanted it to heal scales and muscles, not internal organs or bones — it was only supposed to help me feel less sore after flying all day. I know, I was an idiot, I should have made it more useful."

"And more obvious," Peril said. "What a dopey thing to enchant. It looks like every other rock in the world. If you drop it while you're leaning over a river one day, you'll never find it again."

"It might work on your scar, though," Turtle said to Qibli. He held out the rock and Qibli jumped away from it.

"No way!" he said, touching his snout. "I like my scar! It's part of who I am! Get your magic nonsense away from me."

"Hey," Winter interrupted suddenly. "Where's Foeslayer?"

"Who?" Moon asked.

"I was traveling with a NightWing," he said. "Where'd she go?"

Peril glanced up and realized the big NightWing was no longer in the sky above them. She tried to remember when she'd last seen her — right after the fight? Before Turtle and the others showed up?

"Uh," she said. "I might have told her to go get help."

"Or she might have decided I was dead and left before the same thing happened to her," Winter said bitterly. He stood up in one quick coiling motion. "We needed her! She was going to help us find the lost city of night!"

"The what?" Peril said.

"Hey," Moon said to Winter, trying to nudge him back down. "Maybe don't make any sudden movements until we're sure you're all right. Also, I'm glad you came back, by the way."

"I'm all right," Winter said, stretching his wings and neck again. "It's like it never happened." He turned accusing eyes on Peril, who felt them like little blades of ice stabbing her own eyeballs. "Except that it did. This monster threatened you and then claimed she was here to help you."

"I didn't threaten anyone!" Peril protested. "Not . . . I mean, not *really.*"

"She is here to help us," Turtle said at the same time. "At least, I think so."

"You *think* so?" Peril cried, wounded.

"I mean," he said anxiously, "I guess I wish you hadn't burned Winter, is all . . ."

"It was an accident!" Peril said. "I was trying to get away from him and we crashed —"

"It looked like a fight from what we saw," Qibli said accusingly.

"*Beware the talons of power and fire,*" Moon said softly. "Maybe it *is* her."

Peril looked from one face to another, her heart pounding. "What are you talking about?" she said.

"Moon had a vision — a prophecy," Turtle said.

"About me?" That couldn't be a good sign. If Moon saw Peril in a vision doing terrible things, then maybe Peril's bad side really was going to win out in the end. Maybe it was inevitable. Maybe she shouldn't even try to fight it.

But Clay said . . . Clay believes in me . . . he can't be wrong, *can he?*

"Not specifically about you," Moon said. "I couldn't see any dragon's faces in the vision. But there was one line at the beginning —"

"Excuse me," Winter said. "Are we really going to tell the villain everything we know about their evil plan?"

"I don't have an evil plan!" Peril said, starting to panic. "All my evil is spur-of-the-moment! Turtle, tell them how bad I am at planning."

"Maybe if she knows about the prophecy, she can do something different," Moon said. "We *can* change the future, you know." She turned to Peril and said, "Listen.

Beware the darkness of dragons.
Beware the stalker of dreams.
Beware the talons of power and fire.
Beware one who is not what she seems.
Something is coming to shake the earth.
Something is coming to scorch the ground.
Jade Mountain will fall beneath thunder and ice,
unless the lost city of night can be found."

Peril looked from her to the others. Moon's eyes were glowing as though she was delivering a message from the stars themselves. Her voice got all low and shivery and it was *decidedly creepy.*

"Well?" Moon asked. "What do you think?"

"You think that first part is about me?" Peril said. Was that what Turtle thought, too? Was he just keeping an eye on her in case she started scorching the ground and knocking over mountains? "I don't stalk anyone's dreams. And I'm exactly what I seem like on the outside. Also, sure, I have talons of fire, but no power whatsoever. If I did have any power, my life would be pretty different from what it is now, believe me."

"Death is a power," Winter said. "You carry death in your talons." He lashed his tail, shooting a hard look at Qibli and Moon. "Is this really your new ally? I leave for five days and you start working with a mass murderer?"

"You left pretty firmly," Qibli pointed out. "You said you weren't coming back, so why should you get a vote? Also, she just showed up with Turtle."

"And I can just leave again, too!" Peril cried. It felt as if the thorns were still there, digging under her scales. It felt like another crocodile in the face. If what she had with Turtle was friendship, and this was what came with it, then friends were *so not worth it*. "I don't need this! I don't even want to work with any of you! I can find Scarlet on my own — that's what I wanted to do in the first place anyway!"

She launched herself into the sky.

"Peril!" Turtle shouted. "Wait!"

That was what she'd wanted him to say, but it wasn't enough. It wouldn't be enough even if he could catch up to her — which he couldn't — and even if he apologized for his awful friends and promised he didn't think she was some predestined sinister bad guy.

Which he wouldn't.

Maybe if he told me he'd leave them and just be friends with me . . .

But he wasn't going to do that either.

She wasn't nearly as important to him as his precious winglet.

Well, that was just fine. She'd wasted enough time on him. Now she could get on with finding Queen Scarlet, killing her, and going back to Clay.

Peril set her course for the Claws of the Clouds Mountains, soaring directly over Possibility and beating her wings to fly as fast as she could.

She did *not* look back to see if Turtle tried to follow her.

Well, maybe once. But he wasn't, so it didn't matter.

After some time, though, when Possibility was well in the distance, she became aware of the sound of wingbeats behind her. It seemed highly unlikely that any of those inferiorly winged dragonets could have caught up to her, but she swung around with her dangerous face on just in case.

"Oh!" said the SkyWing behind her, catching air below his wings to stop and hover. And then he smiled. He SMILED. That never happened, not when dragons first met her. WHAT WAS THAT ABOUT?

"What do you want?" Peril demanded. She was pretty sure this was the SkyWing who had flown out of Possibility to meet her, but had run away again once he saw Winter and Foeslayer. Had he been watching for her? Waiting for her to leave them?

"Uh," he said. "Nothing?"

Peril hovered in the air, scrutinizing him. He was big, a lot older than her, with warm orange scales and amber eyes. No scars that she could see, which was unusual for a full-grown SkyWing under Scarlet's reign. Huge powerful wings, long horns with faint golden markings on them. He also looked wealthier than the average SkyWing; there were gold rings on three of his claws, a black necklace with gold spikes circled his throat, and an armband wove like a snake all the way up one of his front legs, with tiny rubies glittering like eyes at one end. He also had a kind of black metal sheath fitted tightly across his chest with a padlock on the outside, perhaps containing more treasure.

She was reasonably certain she'd never seen this particular SkyWing before, although it was equally possible she had and just didn't remember him. Was he one of Queen Scarlet's generals? Maybe he'd been away overseeing soldiers in the war. But then surely he'd have a war wound or two somewhere.

"You're Peril," he said. "Right?"

"You say that like there's actually a chance I'm someone else," Peril said.

"Well," he said, "there's always a chance. Isn't there?"

That was a weird thing to say. She tilted her head at him. "I have no idea who *you* are."

"My name," he said importantly, "is Soar."

"Oh," Peril said. She thought for a moment. "Really? That's . . . unusual."

"Is it?" he asked, deflating.

"Well, yes," she said. "Not very, um — aspirational, I guess."

"But it's a very SkyWing name, right?" he said.

"Why?" she said. "It's not like we get more sore than other dragons. It's probably the other way around, since we're built for flying longer distances —"

"Wait," he broke in. "No, no, no. Not SORE. SOAR, S-O-A-R, like flying high over the kingdom. Oh, good grief. Have other dragons been thinking my name is *Sore* all these years?"

"Probably," Peril said.

"Why are you the first dragon to say anything?" he demanded.

Peril thought for a moment. "Because I'm not polite," she said finally. "No one ever taught me to be. I don't care what dragons think, because they won't like me even if I say all the right things and bow the right way and smile until my snout hurts, so why should I bother?"

"I know what you mean," he said. "You can do and say everything exactly the same as everyone else, but if there's *one thing* different about you, that's all they care about."

"I assume so," Peril said. "I've never actually tried acting like other dragons."

"Well, it doesn't work," he said. Something was glowing in his cycs, an old, old anger. "Trust me. You still end up banished from your own home."

Peril looked at him in surprise. "*You* were banished from the Sky Kingdom, too? When? By Ruby or by Scarlet? What for?"

"It's a long story," he said. "I'll tell you all of it someday. But the short answer is — for being myself. Because I had no choice, back then."

For a moment, Peril wasn't sure whether he felt familiar because she actually knew him, or because he sounded so much like herself.

"You don't need those other dragons," he said. "The ones you were just with. They can't understand you. But I can help you find what you're looking for."

"Oh, really?" Peril said. "Do you even know what that is?"

"I think so," he said. He flashed around her suddenly, heading for the mountains. "Follow me!"

That wasn't terribly convincing, but it wasn't as though Peril had a particularly clear alternate plan anyway.

"I don't like following anyone!" she called. With a flick of her tail, she spun herself around and caught up to fly beside him. "Hey, why haven't I ever met you before?"

"An excellent question," he said. "The only answer I've been able to come to is that Queen Scarlet prefers to keep her toys separate from each other."

"I'm no one's *toy*," Peril hissed, curling her claws in. Why did dragons keep saying that about her and Scarlet? "Anyone who tries to play with me will find that out *very* fast."

He tipped his head in a conciliatory way. "My apologies. I confess I don't see myself that way either. Perhaps it would be more accurate to say Scarlet didn't want her most powerful friends joining forces against her."

Peril snorted a laugh, sending a little burst of flames into the sky. "*You're* one of her most powerful friends? What can you do? Pay enemy dragons to run away?"

"Well," he said, "I doubt Scarlet would consider this useful, but among other things, it appears that I can father dragonets with firescales."

Peril blinked at him. He stared back at her, his amber eyes almost twinkling. He seemed to be waiting for her to collapse in a fit of joy or run around shrieking with delight or something.

"Oh, really?" Peril said. "Do you mean me? Was that your idea of a heartwarming revelation? You're my *father*?"

"Yeeees," he said carefully. "You don't seem very excited about that."

"Why should I believe you?" she demanded. "Where have you been my whole life? Why haven't you ever talked to me before? What are you trying to get out of me now? What made you suddenly decide to say hello?"

"Hey, hey, calm down," he said.

"Yeah, all right, that certainly *sounded* patronizing enough to make you my dad," Peril said. "Do it again. Tell me you know what's best for me. Say something about how I don't really understand the world and you're here to guide me and teach me and help me grow up, because I couldn't possibly do that on my own."

"*Listen*," he said. "I didn't know you were alive. I'm usually away doing . . . things for the queen . . . so I missed the entire episode where Kestrel tried to escape with you and your brother. By the time I returned, Queen Scarlet told me you were dead. She said none of Kestrel's dragonets had survived, and that Kestrel had gone to join the Talons of Peace. Everyone was forbidden to speak of Kestrel, and I had no idea . . . I mean, I knew *you* existed, the dragonet with firescales, but I didn't know you were *my* daughter until a few days ago."

"Well," Peril said. "I bet that came as quite a disappointment."

"Not to me," he said. "My daughter is powerful and amazing and terrifying. Who wouldn't be proud of that?"

Peril sort of wished he'd left the *terrifying* out of that description, but still, it was a weird feeling to be featured in a sentence anywhere near the word "proud."

"So how did you find out?" she asked.

"A, uh . . . a friend told me."

"A friend?" Peril echoed. "He certainly took his time about it."

"He didn't know either," Soar protested. "His name is Cirrus. He's with the Talons of Peace. And when he told me, I had to — I mean, I *immediately* came looking for you. If I'd known sooner . . ." He trailed off.

"You would have what?" Peril asked. "Saved me from the arena? Told me the truth about the black rocks? Stopped Queen Scarlet from using me? Stopped Ruby from banishing me? Could you actually have been useful ever in my life? I'm guessing no."

"I could be useful now," he said. "I can change everything for you."

"I doubt that," Peril said. She twisted into a spiral, arrowing for the gap between the first two mountain peaks. The wind buffeted her wings, trying to knock her off course, but she stayed straight and true through the pass, sweeping up into a mossy valley dotted here and there with doomed sheep.

As the sheep stampeded in alarm and Soar caught up to Peril, she spotted movement in a cluster of trees higher up the slope.

Her breath caught in her throat. She knew that color orange, knew it like a bloodbath of fear and awe sweeping through her.

With slow, majestic wingbeats, a glittering dragon rose out of the trees and plunged toward them.

It was Queen Scarlet.

Peril had found her — or she had found Peril — at last.

CHAPTER 11

"It's the queen," Peril said, squaring her shoulders. "You run. I'll stop her." *That's what I'm here for. This is the moment when I take her down forever. I'll finally use my fire for something that will make Pyrrhia a safer place.*

"Wait," Soar said. "Before you attack her, hear her out."

Peril whirled around and read the betrayal in his face before her mind had even processed his words.

"You're working with her," she growled. "You brought me to her on purpose!"

"Well," he said, "to be fair, that's what she wanted, but it's also what *you* wanted, isn't it? So does that really *count* as a betrayal? I mean, now everyone's happy. So . . . yay, me?"

Queen Scarlet arrived then with a whoosh of hot air, circling maddeningly around Peril and Soar. Peril had forgotten how bad the scar on her face was. The queen looked thin and ragged, but still alight with fury, like a cold flame that would never go out.

"Oh ho," Scarlet called to Soar. "That's a face I haven't seen in a while."

Me? Peril thought. "I've been looking for you," she called back, whipping around to keep the queen in sight. "You can't threaten my friends like that and get away with it."

"Friends?" Queen Scarlet laughed a high, genuine laugh that bounced merrily off the mountain peaks. "Is that what you think Glory is to you, darling? I'm sure she cares about you so very much. Do you think anyone would cry if I'd dropped *your* decapitated head in their talons? Admit it: nobody loves you the way you are except me. That's always been true and it always will be true."

"No, it's not!" Peril cried. "There are other dragons who like me!"

"But wouldn't they all change you if they could?" Scarlet said pityingly. "They would strip away your firescales and squash your lovely craziness into a well-mannered box. Not me, though. I think every inch of you is just perfect."

"As long as I do what you want," Peril pointed out. "The minute I have a thought of my own, you hate me."

"*Oh,*" Scarlet said. "*That* sounds new! Have you had any of these 'thoughts of your own' yet? All I've seen from you so far are those MudWing's thoughts and decisions. If you actually do have one of your very own, I can't wait to hear about it."

"Can you two please stop arguing?" Peril's father inter-jected. He angled down to land on a circle of giant boulders. Peril swooped after him, choosing the barest rock she could find, and Scarlet joined them a moment later.

The three SkyWings glowered at one another for a long moment. At least, Peril and Scarlet were glowering; Soar looked infuriatingly pleased with himself.

"I'm smarter than you think," he said to Queen Scarlet. "I figured it out. You lied to me all these years, but I know the truth now."

"How thrilling for you," she replied with lidded eyes, hissing smoke out her nostrils.

"This is Kestrel's daughter," he said, his voice rising. "*My* daughter." His tail flicked toward Peril's, as though he were tempted to twine it around hers, but stopped at the last moment.

"Yes, I know," Scarlet said. "She certainly is. But you didn't deserve to know. You had no right to do what you did, and so I decided you'd never get to meet the monster that came of it. I'm sure every queen in Pyrrhia would agree with me."

"Why? What did he do?" Peril asked. Her heart felt like a campfire that was about to be stomped out.

Scarlet smirked. "So you still haven't told her. I love it. Acting all indignant and self-righteous about me lying to you! And yet here you are, lying to your own daughter right now. Tsk tsk tsk."

"I'm not agreeing with her," Peril said to Soar. "But I don't like being lied to. What is she talking about?"

"Now is . . . is not the time," Soar said awkwardly. "I'll tell her everything later."

"You don't need to tell her," said the queen. "I'll just go ahead and show her." In a lightning-fast move, she suddenly leaped from her boulder to Soar's, flipped him onto his back, and pinned him to the boulder.

"Stop!" Soar cried, pushing ineffectively at Scarlet's claws.

Peril reared up with her wings flared wide. *This is it. I should kill her. I'd be saving my father. This is the right moment. Even Clay would want me to. Now. Do it now, Peril.*

But . . . what was the truth Scarlet wanted her to know?

And what if she attacked the wrestling dragons and accidentally burned her father as well?

And how could she kill the dragon who'd kept her alive when everyone else wanted her dead?

And what if the queen was right? What if no one else ever did love Peril?

What if killing Scarlet didn't work to change everyone's minds?

What if she made another mistake like she had with Winter, only someone really died, and then even Clay had to hate her, and she got thrown out of Jade Mountain forever, and all the queens in all the kingdoms banished her, and she had nowhere to go and no one else in the world?

Wouldn't she regret killing her queen then? Wouldn't she wish there were *someone* left alive who loved her?

All these thoughts flashed through her head at once, making Peril hesitate long enough to realize that Scarlet wasn't attacking Soar.

The queen was merely holding Soar down while she sliced off the gold-spiked necklace he was wearing. For such a big, strong-looking SkyWing, he was obviously not much of a fighter; he protested, loudly, but barely struggled.

Finally Queen Scarlet was able to rip the leather in two and the choker clattered to the ground, revealing a strip of something small and white tucked into a hidden pocket inside it.

"There," Scarlet said, stepping back with a satisfied toss of her head.

Soar scrambled to his feet, scowling . . . but his eyes were no longer amber . . . and his orange scales were shifting, shrinking and changing color just like the decapitated not-Glory head.

Peril jumped back, leaving scorch marks across the moss on the edge of the rock. *He's not a SkyWing.*

Was he a NightWing? Could he be the NightWing who had followed her and Turtle earlier?

If I'm half NightWing, maybe I have some cool powers I don't know about. Maybe their tribe would take me in — I bet they'd like me, if they could figure out how to use me.

But Soar's scales weren't turning black either.

They were turning . . . green.

Not a rich, dark green like Turtle's scales; in fact, not a color green that Peril had ever seen on any SeaWing before. Soar was now the color of limes and jungle parakeets, a sort of nondescript yellowish-green that clashed horribly with the moss under him. He was also skinnier than he had been before, with narrower shoulders and less shiny teeth. His wings were smaller and his tail . . . his tail coiled in a loop behind him like a monkey's . . . or like a —

"A RainWing?" Peril said. "Seriously. My father is a RainWing. Is this a joke?"

"He's not much of a RainWing," Scarlet said, smirking. "That's why they threw him out. Just like you, actually, banished from his kingdom. Like father, like daughter; no one wants either of you anywhere. Except me, of course. Wouldn't a little gratitude be in order here?"

"So what if I am a RainWing?" Peril's father said to the queen. "When I met Kestrel I was a full SkyWing. She never knew I was anything else. Our dragonets would have been full SkyWings. That's how it works."

"Ha," Scarlet snorted. "You don't know that. I say it's no coincidence this one turned out the way she did. SkyWings should only have eggs with other SkyWings, and here's your proof."

"That's not proof," he snapped. "SkyWings have been having dragonets with firescales for centuries. You can't blame that on me! It has nothing to do with — with who I really am."

"I'm a hybrid?" Peril said, not quite following this conversation. "How can I be half RainWing? I don't look anything like them." She held out her talons and tried to will her scales to change color. When nothing happened, she touched her front fangs, wondering whether they could secretly shoot venom. Not that she needed extra weaponry, but it would be pretty cool anyway.

"You're *not* a hybrid," said her father, a little impatiently considering he was dropping a basket full of crazy on her head. "I was a SkyWing when I met Kestrel and fathered you. You wouldn't have any RainWing characteristics. You're all SkyWing."

"But what are you talking about, you were a SkyWing?" Peril asked. "Turning your scales orange doesn't make you a SkyWing."

"Ha ha ha!" Scarlet laughed. "He can't even do that, my dear."

"No, but I can do other things," he snapped. "I — have a gift, Peril. Look." He picked up the ripped necklace and held it around his neck.

Once more his scales rippled, this time back to orange, and suddenly Soar the SkyWing was standing in front of Peril again.

"See?" he said in his deeper, stronger voice. "I can change my entire self. Now I'm a full SkyWing."

"With a terrible name you gave yourself," Peril guessed. "That explains that. What's your real name?"

"Chameleon," he said, dropping the necklace and turning back into the defensive green dragon. "Some dragons might say that was a cruel irony, while others, for instance an entire tribe of RainWings, might laugh and laugh for days once everyone realizes that the dragon named 'Chameleon' is the only one in the rainforest who can't change his scales."

Peril wasn't particularly interested in his sob stories from the past. Pieces were starting to come together in her head.

"*You're* the one who enchanted the head to look like Glory!" Peril said. "You're helping Queen Scarlet scare my friends!"

"Hey, she pays very well," he said, displaying the rings on his claws. "At least, she *used* to. I've had more treasure than any RainWing in the history of Pyrrhia for years now.

The last several months haven't been quite the same, though." He shot a disapproving look at the queen.

"I'll have my kingdom back soon enough," Queen Scarlet said. "Although I think you owe *me* for the prize you lost a few days ago."

Peril closed her eyes, frowning. This conversation was distracting her from her goal: killing Scarlet.

If that was still the right thing to do. Was it? Queen Scarlet didn't seem so terrifying and monstrous here, in this quiet valley, talking about Peril's lovely craziness and her father.

Remember all the terrible things she's done. That random MudWing she killed to get that head. Sending Clay and his friends to fight in the arena. Forcing my mother to kill my twin brother . . .

But she kept me *alive, when everyone else in the tribe would have had me killed the moment I hatched.*

And she's right — she never wanted to change me. She likes my scales the way they are. I'm not sure even Clay feels that way. She remembered him wincing when he touched her, and the way he watched her wings carefully when she was near anything flammable.

Did Scarlet really have to die?

Oh, Clay, why can't you be here to tell me what's right?

She opened her eyes and looked at Chameleon, who was fiddling with the metal sheath around his chest. This was Scarlet's mysterious new ally. Peril's own father — a disgraced RainWing with strange shape-shifting abilities. He wasn't so terrifying either.

Would it be so bad if Scarlet did get her throne back? What if Ruby agreed to step down, and Scarlet agreed to leave Peril's friends alone, and Peril agreed to stop setting dragons on fire (unless they really deserved it), and everything went mostly back to normal?

"Peril," said Chameleon, breaking into her thoughts. "I know I haven't been a father to you before, but I can change that. I think I can give you a gift that's everything you've always wanted."

"There's nothing I've always wanted," Peril said. The image of Clay wrapping his wings around her and never letting go flashed through her head, but she shoved it away. She was a long way off from getting that, or deserving it, or feeling as if she could accept it even if Clay ever — *stop thinking about this,* she ordered herself.

"Oh, really?" Chameleon pulled out a thick chain of silvery-black metal links, with a black locket dangling from one end of it. Peril recognized the metal as the kind Scarlet used to bind the wings and ankles of her prisoners; impervious to most dragon fire, but not to Peril's. Carved on the outside of the locket was a dragon shape, wings spread and tail curled in two loops below, inlaid with a golden-copper metal that glinted in the sunlight like Peril's scales.

Peril regarded it for a moment. "You're right," she said. "All my life I have desperately wanted an ugly necklace."

"Hey," Chameleon protested, as Queen Scarlet gave a shout of laughter.

"Especially one that will melt the moment I put it on," Peril said. "Thank you *soooooo* much! Best dad ever."

"This is the kind of parenting fun you've missed out on," Scarlet said to him. "You're welcome."

"It's not just a necklace," Chameleon insisted, ignoring Scarlet. "Peril, don't you understand what I can do? I can turn you into anyone you want. I could make you a SeaWing or an IceWing or even a scavenger, if you particularly wanted to get eaten for some reason. I could make you a MudWing. I can *take away your firescales*. Don't you see? You could be normal. You could be a dragon who can touch other dragons. You don't have to be this monster everyone is afraid of. I can change you."

Peril stared at him, wondering if her scales were floating off into the clouds the way it felt like they might be.

"I thought your power was only meant to be used for special cases," Scarlet mused. "Something about consequences and risks and something blah."

"This is a special case," Chameleon said. "I'd do anything for my dragonet."

"Aww," Scarlet said sarcastically. "What a rare and unusual parent." Something seemed to strike her and she inhaled a plume of smoke, turning her head to gaze thoughtfully toward the north.

"You're serious," Peril said to her father. "This is real? I put that necklace on and I won't be me anymore?" She couldn't figure out how she felt about that. It sounded glorious and awful at the same time. No more Peril. *No more Peril.* Everyone would be safe from her forever. *But without my firescales, who am I?*

"It's up to you," he answered. "This particular necklace is only enchanted to take away your firescales. You'll still be you, the same Peril, with all your own personality and history. But you'll have normal SkyWing scales and you'll be able to touch whoever you want without hurting them. Can you imagine? You'd be a regular dragon. But if you want a different enchantment, turning you into someone else entirely, I could do that, too."

I could be a MudWing. Someone Clay could be with and love without anyone hating me for it. They don't even need to know that I used to be Peril.

Except for him — I need him to know who I really am. I'd have to tell him about this transformation as myself first. I could be Peril for now — safe Peril, no firescales, no danger to anyone. And then after I talk to him, I could become whoever he wants. Clay could decide! He could imagine the perfect dragon for himself, and that's what I could become. Exactly what he wants in every detail. Then he would have to love me, wouldn't he?

She started to reach for the necklace, then pulled back. "It won't work," she said. "That necklace will melt and fall apart the moment it touches my scales."

"This metal is thick and strong," Chameleon said. "And the transformation only takes a moment. I think it will last until your scales are safe, if you put it on quickly. It's worth a try, isn't it? And if it doesn't work, we'll make something else. But if it does work, don't take it off — the more times it goes on and off, the more chances there are of destroying it."

Peril hesitated one last time. "This isn't a trick, right? I'll still be myself?"

"Of course," said Chameleon. "Just like I am always myself, but each of my faces is a better version of me. You'll be Peril, but finally a Peril that dragons can love."

And if it is a trick, Peril thought, *and I disappear . . . would it be such a great loss for the world? Would Clay even miss me? Wouldn't Turtle be happy never to see me again?*

She snatched the necklace from Chameleon's claws and

dropped it over her head, over her horns, until it landed around her neck, the locket hitting her chest with a thump.

She waited for it to curl into a molten mess.

But it didn't.

Nothing happened.

Actually nothing. It just sat there. Peril felt exactly the same.

She poked the necklace. Nothing, just a necklace, hanging around her neck, ostentatiously NOT melting.

"How do you feel?" Chameleon asked.

Peril looked up to find both of them squinting at her. She held out her talons to examine them.

"Do I look any different?"

"Not much," said Chameleon.

"Less incandescent," said Scarlet. "More disappointing. More . . . *ordinary.*" She spat out the last word like a rotten pear, but it sounded beautiful to Peril.

"Really?" Peril turned and saw a small yellow flower growing out of a crack in the boulder she sat on. She slowly reached out one claw, her whole arm trembling, and brushed the petals.

The flower wobbled. The flower bent with Peril's claw, slipped back to its place, and fluttered its yellowness cheerfully in the wind.

The flower lived.

"Did you see that?" Peril gasped.

"Yawn," said Scarlet.

Peril poked the flower again, and when it still didn't burst into flame, she leaped off the boulder entirely, landing on all fours in the grass below.

The grass lived!

Peril ran full-out across the meadow, stomping her talons into the grass, flicking branches with her wings, rolling in patches of ivy, ramming her side into trees.

Everything lived!

She startled a sheep out of its hiding place in a cave and it galloped across her path, bleating with shaggy terror. Delighted, Peril thwacked it with her tail, sending it bouncing across the grass several feet. It leaped up and kept running away, and a grin the size of Jade Mountain spread across Peril's face.

"Look at me!" she shouted to her father and her queen. She grabbed a tree with her front talons and shook it until a mortified squirrel fell out. "I can do anything!"

"Except wreak fiery vengeance on my enemies," Queen Scarlet muttered grumpily.

Peril skipped back across the grass to them, settling herself on top of the most flammable patch of foliage she could find. And it survived! Nothing was on fire in this whole entire valley! This was the most beautiful place in the world!

"Don't worry," she said to the queen, breathing a small spurt of perfectly normal dragonflame from her mouth. "We can still do that. The vengeance, enemies, whatever thing. Where do you want to start?"

Queen Scarlet sat up and looked at her. Then she looked at Chameleon. He bowed deeply, his wings spread wide.

"At your service, Your Majesty," he said with a smile.

"I do have one great idea," Queen Scarlet said, regarding Peril thoughtfully.

"Then what are we waiting for?" Peril asked. "Let's go get your kingdom back."

Ice Kingdom

Sky Kingdom

Queen Thorn's
Stronghold

Claws of the
Clouds Mountains

Kingdom of
Sand

Scorpion Den

Jade Mountain

PART THREE

A NEW PERIL

—— CHAPTER 12 ——

They flew north immediately, as darkness began to stretch across the mountains below them and the tiny heartbeats of stars started to flicker in the sky. Peril felt light, lighter than she thought she'd ever felt before. She was like smoke on the wind, like a drift of dandelion seeds. She was free.

I have nothing to worry about anymore.

She did a flip in the air, swooped up behind her father — who was back in his SkyWing shape as Soar, although somehow without his ripped necklace; that was weird, she should ask him how he'd done that later; probably by enchanting something else, whatever, no big deal — and tackled him so he toppled sideways and had to do a funny frantic flapping spiral to recover.

Peril laughed and laughed. "I've never been able to do that to anyone before!" she cried. "I've always wanted to tackle someone in midair!" She zoomed around him and nudged one of his wings heartily with one of hers, unbalancing him again. "And that! I've always wanted to do that!"

"Could you perhaps save some of your affectionate impulses for when I'm not fighting an updraft?" Chameleon asked, ducking out of her way as she dive-bombed him again. "I mean, I love it, thank you, but it's a little vigorous for night flying, for me."

"You're the best," Peril said. She couldn't stop herself from bodychecking him in the side again. "That was the last time, I promise!" she called as he reeled away. "Because when we get to the Sky Palace, there will be lots of dragons to do this to! I'm going to nudge wings and poke tails and HUG EVERYONE!"

"No," Queen Scarlet said sharply. She swung around and lined herself up to fly alongside Peril. "You can't do that. Not until I have the throne back. No one can know that you're powerless now — I need the threat of you, which should be as effective as the actual fire of you, after the last seven years. Once we've secured the throne and I've killed Ruby, then you can be as dippy and cuddly and stupid as you want."

"Oh," Peril said, her light dimming a little. She had been hoping for a triumphant return as Safe Peril, Ordinary Peril, one of you, a regular SkyWing who can totally just be part of the tribe now, let's be friends, hooray!

But Queen Scarlet had a point. She needed Peril's help, and that's what Peril was here for, after all.

"All right," Peril said with a flick of her tail. "It won't take long to make you queen again anyway."

"You'll have to pay attention," said the queen. "Don't do anything stupid. Act exactly as you always have and don't touch anything. In fact, don't say anything either. Just stand there and look menacing."

"I can do that!" Peril said cheerfully. "I'll practice my menacing face right now. *Rrrrgh. Hrrgrrrrmbrrgh. Rrrroarrrrg.*"

"You sound like you're digesting an overweight grizzly bear," Scarlet commented acidly.

"I think it's perfect," said Chameleon.

"Thanks, Dad," Peril said, grinning.

"Dragonets," Scarlet muttered. "I never saw the appeal." The Sky Palace came into view ahead of them, its towers and turrets and spires jutting through the clouds around the mountain peaks like long spindly claws. The fading sunlight seemed to catch for a moment in the queen's eyes, adding a glimmer of menace to her yellow gaze as she regarded the palace.

"That's why this never occurred to me before," she went on. "But I should have remembered . . . it was only a couple of months before the whole catastrophe."

Chameleon cleared his throat and the queen glanced at him, trading some kind of significant unspoken message.

"Won't there be guards?" Chameleon asked quickly. "Patrolling around the mountains?"

"Not as many as there would be if Ruby were home," Queen Scarlet said. "But she's still off hunting for me and trying to identify missing heads. It's the perfect opportunity to take over . . . and get the leverage I need to keep it that way."

Two SkyWings suddenly emerged from the mist, flapping toward them with spears clutched in their talons and fearsome scowls etched on their snouts.

"Still," Chameleon said, "um . . . *any* guards seems like a problem, right?"

"Not for us," Queen Scarlet said, tossing her head triumphantly at Peril. "Let's go, darling."

Darling! Peril thought with delight as she soared up behind the queen. *That's me. She does love me!*

The two guards lifted their spears when they saw Queen Scarlet approaching — but a moment later they saw Peril, and she saw them recognize her, and she saw the fear that engulfed them. One dropped his spear and turned tail instantly, fleeing back to the palace as fast as his wings could carry him. The other hovered indecisively for a moment, shifting her weapon from talon to talon and flicking her tail like a leaf about to be blown off a tree. Then she, too, broke down and fled.

Peril watched them go, feeling hurt and lonely and misunderstood exactly the way she always had, and trying to reach for that part of her that was too fierce and scary to care.

But it's different now, she told herself. *It'll all be different once they know that I'm normal. Maybe we'll even be friends. That would be cool; I've never had a real friend before.*

Something poked at the corners of her mind. *Oh — that SeaWing. Turtle. I guess he was sort of a friend, apart from lying to me.*

She realized that she should tell Queen Scarlet that the SeaWings had an animus. That was definitely the kind of thing the queen would want to know, plus it would be pretty impressive to be the dragon who got to tell her such an important and surprising secret.

She twisted toward the queen, but Scarlet was already in a dive, aiming for an opening high in one of the towers. It was a room Peril had never been to, as far as she could remember, and she flew after Scarlet, puzzling over what it could be.

If she'd had a normal dragonethood, she might have been able to guess from the murmur of little voices that came through the windows.

Then again, if she'd had a normal dragonethood, she'd have spent most of it right here.

They swooped through the highest opening of the tower, straight into an enormous space full of SkyWing dragonets.

The wingery, Peril realized. *Of course I'd never have been allowed in here. Staying out of the way of clumsy, floppy dragonets was always the hardest thing about moving around the palace.* In fact, the danger of running into Peril was probably why most dragonets were confined to the wingery until they had better control of their limbs.

The youngest dragonets were play-fighting on the floor, far below Peril, near the base of the tower, where black and gold rugs overlapped. Toy weapons were scattered around them, blunt spears and dented shields leaning haphazardly against balls and attack dummies and what appeared to be toy cooking supplies stacked with bits of half-chewed goat bones and other snacks.

Slightly older dragonets swarmed the walls and climbing structures above the rugs, clambering busily along fake rocky outcroppings and jumping to gradually higher and higher platforms. A few of them slipped and fell, but the padded rugs below caught them without injury.

At the highest levels, closer to the ceiling, was space for flying practice — longer spaces to cross with each leap, ropes to catch on midflight, obstacles to practice swerving around. Here the biggest dragonets stretched their wings, red and orange swerving around one another as they cat-called and showed off new moves.

They all seemed so *happy*. Not just happy — unworried. Like nothing could trouble them, like all they needed was a place to fly and friends to fly with.

What would I be like if I'd grown up in this wingery? Peril wondered. *Would I have friends? Would I giggle like that?*

The memory of Turtle tugged at her again and she shook it off. She'd known him for, what, four days? That hardly counted as true friendship. He was probably glad she was gone.

The walls in here were not as embellished with gold and jewels as the rest of the palace; Peril wondered if Queen Scarlet didn't trust dragonets to keep their grubby claws off her treasure. Instead, the room was full of light and air from windows and skylights, most of which were barred — especially on the lower levels — so none of the crawlers or new fliers could fall out.

The only decoration was a portrait of Scarlet five times the size of the actual queen. It covered a huge swathe of wall, forcing dragonets to find ways to climb or flap around it. Queen Scarlet's perfect orange scales, bright yellow eyes, and cascades of jewelry glowed over the whole wingery, as if she were approving of their play while also imprinting their young brains with the constant reminder that she was the queen (and always would be, hinted her expression).

In fact, it was surprising that Ruby hadn't taken that down yet, Peril reflected. Perhaps the interior design of her palace wasn't quite as high a priority for her as it had been for her mother.

Look how beautiful Scarlet was, Peril thought. She glanced at the disfiguring scar Glory had left on the queen's face and gave a little shudder of pity.

Glory . . . how did she get to the queen? What was I doing when that happened? How did I fail her?

Queen Scarlet swooped to a perch at the peak of the tower, on a winding branch carved from wood. It twisted across the roof as though it was the finish line for all the dragonets trying to reach the top of the room. Peril wanted to sit on it herself — her wings were starting to get tired — but she remembered that she was still supposed to be all firescales, so instead she made herself hover just below the queen.

A hush fell over the wingery — very slowly, as several dragonets were too busy playing to notice either the growing quiet or the giant dragon glowering from above.

But Queen Scarlet waited, smoke hissing from her snout and ears.

As they noticed her, many of the dragonets let out squeals of fear. A few of them near the floor dove under whatever they could reach, hiding their faces behind shields or rugs or goat-spattered saucepots, although their trembling tails were still stuck out in the open.

A few of the others began to whisper . . .

"Is that the dragon in the picture?"

"That's not the old missing queen, is it?"

"What wrong with her face?"

"She don't look like her picture."

"How'd she get all meltedish?"

"That's really gross. Gross like Cardinal drooling when he sleeps."

"Shut up!"

"Way grosser than that."

"I wish *my* face was all melty and scary!"

"Ew, you do not, we would so never play with you if it was."

"But you'd be scared of me and then I could creep up on anyone in the dark and give them nightmares forever! It would be awesome!"

"Yuck. I bet she can't even look in mirrors anymore."

"My mom said she used to be wicked scary."

"And kind of mean, not like Queen Ruby."

"She look kind of meanish now, I thinking."

"Should we be more scared?"

Gradually the whispers, too, fell silent under Queen Scarlet's withering glare.

"Hello, dragonets," she finally hissed. "I am your queen — Queen Scarlet of the SkyWings. I have returned to take my throne, but I need something from you. Some*one*, actually."

"Excuse me," a little voice piped up. "I thinking maybe you in the wrong palace maybe? We already has a queen. Queen Ruby, she super-nice."

"Ruby is not your queen," Scarlet snarled. "She is an imposter! *I* am your queen!"

"What's a nimposser?" asked another voice.

"It's furry and sleeps upside down and has a really chewy tail," said another. "Melty-Face, ma'am, you's wrong, Ruby's not furry at all. An' I bet her tail's not chewy either but I hasn't checked."

"She's a very nice queen," offered yet another dragonet, "and she visits all the time and knows all our names and says sorry when she bumps into someone and brings us snacks and we like her lots."

"Maybe you could be queen of someone else?" a small orange dragonet suggested. " 'Cause we already gots a good one but I hears that there's some NightWings maybe lookin' for a new queen? And maybe because they spooky, too, maybe they like your spooky face?"

"Oo, yes," a few others agreed. "She'd be super-good spooky! They could change their name to SpookyWings or NightmareFaces!"

"STOP TALKING THIS INSTANT," Queen Scarlet bellowed. Peril was finding it close to impossible to keep a straight face. She wished there had been a chorus of impertinent dragonets around for every conversation she'd ever had with the queen. Perched on the windowsill, Chameleon wasn't even trying to hide how his shoulders were shaking with laughter.

"Sheesh," one of the little voices muttered as they subsided. "Jus' makin' some helpful *suggestibles*, no need to be crankmonstery."

"I am looking," Queen Scarlet said, cold and clear, with iron in her voice, "for a dragonet named Cliff."

Now everyone really was silent. The SkyWing dragonets glanced around uneasily, and then gradually one head after another turned toward a small, dark red dragon with a long neck who was clinging to a platform near the ground. He looked no more than eight or nine months old.

He stared up at Queen Scarlet and Peril, his tiny claws trembling. Suddenly Peril didn't feel like laughing anymore.

A grim smile spread across Queen Scarlet's face.

"Hello, little prince," she said. "I thought it was time for you to meet your grandmother."

CHAPTER 13

Prince Cliff was by far the teeniest dragon Peril had ever been this close to. If she hadn't known that her scales were safe to touch, she would never have dared to stand so close, no matter what Queen Scarlet's orders were. She tried to wink at him in a friendly way, but she must have done it wrong — friendly winks weren't exactly something she'd ever had a chance to practice — since it just made him throw his wings over his head and curl into a shivering ball.

She didn't love that. She wanted to hug him — she could hug dragons now! — and tell him not to be scared, that she wasn't scary at all, not anymore. But she had her orders, and she couldn't ruin Queen Scarlet's plan, not when it was working so well.

They'd marched the dragonet out of the wingery and down the long winding tunnels with SkyWings scattering in panic before them. Three guards had tried to resist, standing firm at the entrance to the throne room. But when Peril stepped toward them with her talons outstretched, one outright fainted with terror, and the other two were distracted long enough for Scarlet to leap forward and kill them.

"Much better," Scarlet said with satisfaction, shoving the bodies to the side of the door and then setting all three guards on fire. The one who was only unconscious woke up screaming, but the screams didn't last very long.

Chameleon herded Cliff into the throne room and plunked him on the lower visitors' throne, which Burn had often used during alliance meetings. Queen Scarlet swarmed onto her own throne, the tall column carved in the shape of clouds that sat in the center of nearly all Peril's memories of her. Queen Scarlet, issuing orders. Queen Scarlet, scolding Peril for whatever new thing she'd done wrong. Queen Scarlet, choosing who would die under Peril's talons today.

The queen poked at her throne for a few minutes, sniffing with disgust as though she could smell traces of Ruby on it, and then she settled herself majestically and stared out the open wall opposite her. From up there, Peril knew, the queen could see a sweeping view of her kingdom, the Claws of the Clouds Mountains scratching the sky all the way to the far horizon.

"Stand next to the prince," Scarlet ordered Peril. "Close enough to grab him if anyone comes in."

Cliff whimpered and tried to make himself smaller.

"I remember when you hatched," Queen Scarlet said to the little red dragonet. "It was like someone had woken up Ruby for the first time in years. I'm afraid your mother has always been very, very boring. No spark in her at all, which of course is why I allowed her to live. But when she saw you for the first time, suddenly there *were* sparks. You'd think your scales were plated with gold and you'd crawled out with sapphires wrapped around your tail. I can understand a dragon getting excited about treasure, but *that* excited about an ordinary dragonet? It was very weird. You are merely ordinary, aren't you, little grandson? I can tell."

"No," Cliff said suddenly, sitting up and puffing out his chest. "I is *not*."

Scuffling and stamping sounds came from the hall outside the throne room, as if a couple of dragons were trying to put out the last of the fire. The queen watched with narrow eyes as a dragon with bright red scales edged inside and threw himself into a deep bow before her.

"Mother!" he said with a little too much enthusiasm.

She kept her gaze fixed on him, smoke rising from her nostrils.

"Your Majesty!" he added quickly. "You're alive! You've returned! What a, uh — what a glorious day for the Sky

Kingdom! We're all so, so, so, uh, blessed and lucky and *relieved*! Yes. This is thrilling, it really is."

"Vermilion," said the queen, and Peril shivered. The weight of the fury in that one word — Peril hoped she'd never have to hear Scarlet say "Peril" like that. She might as well have called her son "Disappointment."

"A great day," he said, his voice hiccupping over the words. He threw a confused look at Peril, as if he didn't expect to see her there, which was odd because where else would she be? "So . . . great."

"Tell me, Vermilion," the queen growled. "Why exactly did you allow your sister to steal MY throne?"

"Steal — she —" he stammered. "I didn't — we thought —"

"Did you *really* think I was dead?" Queen Scarlet sat up and spread her wings so she loomed over the whole space. "Me?"

"Y-y-yes?" he tried, his expression clearly indicating that he wasn't sure which answer would get him killed faster.

"Really," she said. "Oh, never mind the dreams, is that it? Every night for MONTHS, I came to you. I told you where I was. I told you to send an army for me. Then after I escaped from Burn, I told you to meet me. I told you to form a plan to get my throne back. I told you to kill your sister. Did you do *even one of those things*, Vermilion?"

Yikes, Peril thought. She remembered the nightly visits from Scarlet, full of guilt and rage and expectations. It hadn't occurred to her that Queen Scarlet might be using the dream-visitor to stalk other dragons besides her. Poor Vermilion.

"But — I didn't know it was real," he protested weakly. "Could have been my, um . . . subconscious."

"You mean your guilty conscience?" Queen Scarlet snapped. "Except I *told* you about the dreamvisitor. I followed you through every normal dream you had. Every night you promised to do as I commanded."

"And then I woke up," he said miserably, "and it seemed crazy to obey a dream . . ."

"Or a queen who wasn't right in front of you," Scarlet guessed. "Because it was easier to be a coward, and obey my little mouse daughter, and hope I never came back, rather than to be loyal to your true queen."

"I'm sorry." Vermilion dropped his head and his wings drooped to the floor. "I know you're going to kill me. Or would you rather have me kill myself?"

"Not just yet," Scarlet said, flicking her tail. "I want to know what Ruby has ruined in my absence. It looks like she's been prying my treasure right out of the walls in here."

Peril glanced around and realized the queen was right. The throne room used to have so much gold inlaid in the walls that stepping inside on a bright day would give you an instant headache. At least half of that gold was gone now, leaving only wisps of cloud shapes here and there.

"Um," said Vermilion. "Yes. About that."

"Or was it other dragons stealing from me?" Queen Scarlet guessed. "As soon as they thought I was gone and they knew a weakling was in power — did they immediately start stripping the bones of the palace?"

"No, no," Vermilion said. "No one did that! It was Ruby. She took the gold and used it to, uh — she —"

"Spit it out," the queen hissed.

"She turned your arena into a hospital," he blurted. "She pardoned all the prisoners and brought in doctors and healers from other tribes to teach ours everything they know and she made space for all the wounded soldiers from the war and she's been finding them all places to live and jobs to do and using the gold for all of that."

A long silence followed. Queen Scarlet flicked her tongue out and in, regarding Vermilion with slitted yellow eyes.

"You like her," she said suddenly. "You think Ruby is a good queen."

"No!" he protested, flapping his wings with alarm. "Never! You're the only good queen! I liked my arena job! It's absolutely terrible here now! We always loved all the, uh, the fighting! We missed you so much!"

"Hmmm," said the queen. "Well, luckily your opinion counts for nothing. The throne is mine again now, and Ruby can either accept that or fight me and die." She cast a sideways glance at Prince Cliff, and a serpentine grin slipped across her face. "When is my hapless daughter scheduled to return?" she asked.

"Tomorrow morning," said Vermilion. "She sent an advance messenger."

"Excellent." Queen Scarlet tapped her claws on the edge of the throne. "I think I'll wait for her right here. Vermilion, make an effort to be useful and send up food from the kitchens." She hesitated, then added with a growl, "Perhaps it's worth noting to anyone involved that Prince Cliff will be tasting everything before I eat it."

Oh, Peril thought. *She's afraid of being poisoned? She never was before . . .*

Vermilion bowed again and stumbled out the door in his haste to be gone.

The night wore on with a procession of SkyWings skittering through the throne room, bowing and scraping and apologizing and extolling the wonders of Scarlet's return. But Peril couldn't help thinking there should be more of them. The halls were quieter than she remembered them being, and there was a general hush over the palace, as if half the dragons were in hiding, waiting for something to change.

Waiting for Ruby to return, presumably — waiting to see what would happen and who would win.

The ones who came in were betting on Scarlet, hoping that by throwing themselves at her feet right away, they'd be safe and perhaps even elevated in her renewed regime. Peril could see Queen Scarlet assessing them each, filing their faces away in her memory. Five of the biggest dragons were assigned to stand guard, filling the throne room the way it had always been filled.

And yet . . . Peril was sure she wasn't the only one in here wondering how deep each SkyWing's loyalty really went.

At least she has me, she thought. She stretched out her talons to look at them, feeling pleased. *It'll be worth it eventually, all these looks of hatred I keep getting, because soon they'll know this new me. Soon Queen Scarlet will be back in power, safe and sound, and I can start changing everyone's minds about me.*

Still, there was something unsettling about the looks, as though her scales were thinner now that they weren't firescales.

Or maybe the looks were different. There was something about them that said *betrayal* and *backstabber* where before it had just been normal fear.

Strange. Maybe she was imagining things.

Long after midnight, Queen Scarlet curled her tail in and fell asleep on her throne. Peril's father, too, was already asleep, his big orange wings flopped out on the floor on the far side of the throne from Peril and Cliff.

The little prince was not asleep, though. He was tracing his claws along the grooves in the rock below him, singing softly to himself. At one point he sat up, looked up at the sleeping queen, and then glanced hopefully at Peril.

"Sorry," she said, hoping her voice sounded kind, although to her ears it mostly sounded drippy. "I'm under orders to stay awake all night. Which means not letting you escape."

He looked down at his claws again. "OK." He poked the rock once more, then raised his giant eyes to her again. They were sort of the color of goldfish, a golden orange that was much prettier than Scarlet's yellow eyes. "Want to hear a song?" he whispered.

"A song?" Peril said. "Really?"

"I made it up myself just nowish," he said.

"All right, but quietly," said Peril. "The queen would really hate to be woken up."

"The quee — oh, you mean Grandmother," he said.

Peril stifled a laugh. She didn't think anyone had ever dared call Queen Scarlet "grandmother" before.

"Ready?" Prince Cliff flipped his wings back and stretched his long neck theatrically. "You the audience, so listen up:

We the dragons of the sky
We can fly and fly and fly
We go up so super high
We the dragons of the sky
And we know my mom is best
Better queen than all the rest
She come save us from this mess
We the dragons dragons dragons of the sky!"

Peril arched her brows at him. Cliff gave her a cheeky smile. "What you think?" he asked.

"I think maybe don't sing that song to your grandma," Peril suggested.

"I think maybe mess and rest don't rhyme so right," he said. "Test. West. Vest! Hmmm. I'm a good rhymer, Mommy says so."

"You don't seem all that scared anymore," said Peril.

"Yeah," he said with a small flick of his dark red tail. "Because Uncle Vermilion said Mommy's coming in the morning, and she makes everything better no matter what."

Peril wondered if she could actually collapse around the chasm that had suddenly yawned in her chest. *She makes everything better.* Peril had never felt that way about anyone. Queen Scarlet kept her alive, gave her a purpose, valued her . . . but made things better? No. Mostly Peril's days were made worse whenever she encountered the queen.

So why do you follow her? whispered a tiny part of her brain.

Because what choice do I have? Peril whispered back. *Who else am I going to follow? No one else wants me.*

"Grandma's kind of mean," Cliff observed, watching Peril's face closely. "Mommy said she was but I thought she couldn't be because no one is ever mean to me but then she really was, did you see?"

"What did you think was so mean?" Peril asked curiously.

"She said I's *ordinary*!" Cliff drew himself up to his full tiny height, looking outraged. "Me! I never! So mean!"

"What's so bad about being ordinary?" Peril opened and closed her talons again, feeling her new secret prickle along her palms. "Sounds great to me."

"WHAT?" Cliff's voice was loud enough to make Queen Scarlet stir in her sleep and Peril shushed him quickly. He lowered himself into a crouch and whispered furiously, "Mommy says I'm special. *Everyone* say it. I be number one most beautiful singer in Pyrrhia one day! Friends with every dragon in the whole world! Mommy thinks I can do anything and great things and all things!"

"Wow," Peril said. "Friends with *every* dragon?"

"Yup," Cliff said proudly. "I gotta practice my 'no, no, leave me alone' face, or else everyone want to be with me ALLLLLLS the time."

"Don't wish to be alone," Peril advised. "Alone is awful."

"Yeah," he said. "Probably. Better than ordinary, though."

She shook her head. "You're a weird little dragonet."

Cliff's eyes were hopeful again. "So . . . maybe escape now then?" He sidled toward the edge of the throne.

"Nope, no, sorry," Peril said, waving him back. "We wait for your mother. And then she won't be queen anymore — you know that, right?"

He hummed a line of his song. "We see." He paced around the top of the throne for a moment before finally lying down and then, at last, quietly singing himself to sleep.

Peril did not sleep. She watched the stars creep slowly across the night sky; she watched a distant meteor streak between two of the moons; she watched the little prince's breath rise and fall in small puffs of smoke. She watched the sun slide and sprawl lazily across the mountain peaks as it rose, and very soon after sunrise, she saw the shapes of a wing of dragons flying toward them at full speed.

Ruby knows, Peril guessed. *Someone snuck out to warn her.*

"Your Majesty," she whispered to the queen. "Ruby is coming."

Queen Scarlet was awake in an instant. She ran her talons over her spikes and flexed her claws. She made sure her jewelry was all adjusted perfectly. For a moment her talons hovered over her scarred face, as if she wanted to tear it off, but then they dropped and she lifted her chin, glowering defiantly out at the approaching dragons.

It wasn't long before they swooped in through the opening — Ruby and more guards than Peril could count in a glance. But Ruby was in the lead, landing in a run that brought her nearly to the foot of the thrones before the five guards stepped in her way.

"Mommy!" Cliff cried. He leaped up, waving his wings joyfully.

"Not another step," Queen Scarlet said in a voice of pure ice. "Or you know exactly what will happen to your precious dragonet."

CHAPTER 14

Ruby stood frozen, quivering with fury. The guards standing between her and the thrones had their shoulders hunched, a kind of shame sketched in the shape of their wings. But she wasn't glaring at them or even at Scarlet. The full force of her anger was directed at Peril, who stood a step behind the prince.

"If you touch him —" Ruby choked out. "If you *dare* —"

"She won't unless I tell her to," said the queen imperiously. "But believe me, she will, the moment I give the order."

Huh, Peril thought. *Would I? If I still had firescales . . . and Scarlet ordered me to burn the prince . . . what would I do?*

He's so little.

And I don't kill dragons anymore, rang a different kind of note inside Peril's mind, familiar and unfamiliar at the same time.

She blinked. *Don't I? Why not?*

"I *knew* it," Ruby spat. "I *knew* you couldn't be trusted, you firescales monster."

"I'm just following orders," Peril protested. "She was queen first, you know. And she didn't *banish* me or wish me dead, unlike some dragons. I don't know why you'd expect me to be loyal to you instead."

"I don't want your loyalty!" Ruby shouted. "But this — threatening innocent dragonets? Helping *her*, after everything? That's not exactly the great peaceful new dragon you were claiming to be, is it? I *knew* you were lying. You have always been the reason for everything that's wrong with the Sky Kingdom."

"Me?" Peril cried, astonished. Ruby really did hate her more than anyone else; Peril wasn't just being paranoid. But why? "I just do what I'm told! Like everyone else! I kill Queen Scarlet's enemies, that's all! What did I ever do to *you*?"

"Excuse me," said Queen Scarlet from the top of her throne. "I feel like we're getting off topic. *I'm* the one who's here to take back the kingdom."

"Those eggs on the brightest night," Ruby said, clutching the floor. Behind her, Peril saw several of her guards nodding, frowning, remembering something awful and hating Peril for it when Peril couldn't even remember it herself . . . or could she? She saw a flash of white eggshells turning to black between her talons, here in this very room.

What did I do? What did Scarlet make me do?

"And my sister," Ruby hissed. "Do you even remember her, among the hundreds of dragons you've killed?"

Peril stared at her for a long moment, wracking her brain. "No," she said finally. "Who?"

Ruby shrieked a long scream of rage, so apparently that was the wrong thing to say.

But high up on her cloud throne, Queen Scarlet was laughing.

"Oh, *Ruby*," she said, shaking her head. "Ruby, you empty-headed princess. Is that what you've thought all these years? Have you been hating my poor little champion for the one terrible thing she actually *didn't* do?"

A blistering hush swept over the throne room. Ruby was looking at her mother now, confusion starting to ebb between the lines of fury in her expression.

"What?" she said finally.

"Peril didn't kill Tourmaline," Queen Scarlet said airily. "She's not even dead, actually."

"She's not?" said Ruby. "Where is she?"

"Let's try to focus, shall we?" said the queen. "I'm here for my throne. Thank you for keeping it warm for me, but it's time to give it back."

"Mommy," Cliff called. "Mommy, I have to tell you something. Mommy! Grandma is kind of mean."

"I know, sweetheart, don't worry," Ruby said. She clenched her jaw, fixing her eyes on her mother again. "You can't have the throne back. You can't just saunter in here and claim it after being gone for months. A queen who abandons her throne has abdicated it forever."

"Oh, really?" Scarlet said. "I don't believe this question has ever come up in the Sky Kingdom before. So where did that convenient rule come from?"

Ruby lifted her chin, her eyes burning. "I decreed it. As queen."

"Aha. I sssee," said Scarlet. She leaned over the edge of her throne, arching her neck as a little burst of flames curled from her nose. "Then *as queen*, I *un*decree it. What are you going to do about that?"

"I am the queen," Ruby said firmly. "And you can't challenge me for it. Only sisters, daughters —"

"Yes yes yes blah blah blah," Scarlet said, waving one talon in the air. "But my dear, you can quote rules at me all day long and it won't change one particular important fact. I have your son."

Ruby looked down at Prince Cliff again. He waved timidly, and she made a little gesture with her shoulders, which seemed to be a quiet signal to sit up and look brave, because that was what he did next.

Peril felt a brief, wild impulse to pick up the dragonet and throw him to the safety of his mother's arms. *I can't do that. That would really ruin everything for my queen.*

But is it the right thing to do? came that strange whisper again, as though her mind was haunted by some other version of herself. She poked one claw into her ear, scratching as if she could drag it out and examine it.

"So really there's only one question," said Queen Scarlet with all the self-important glee that had ever been mustered in Pyrrhia. "Which would you rather have — the throne or your dragonet?"

"Your Majesty," said one of the dragons behind Ruby, and it took Peril a moment to realize he was talking to Ruby and not Scarlet. "We can fight. We *will* fight for you. Your supporters outnumber hers and we're more loyal."

"I know," said Ruby. "But a hundred thousand SkyWings still couldn't save Cliff in the next minute, if my mother sets her creature on him." Peril felt the sting of Ruby's bitterness from across the room, the confirmation that once again, Peril had ruined everything for her.

I'm just being who I am, Peril thought.

Although I'm not a creature anymore, actually. I'm only pretending to be dangerous for Queen Scarlet. So I'm not really being my new self at all.

But I promised to be loyal to her. Isn't that an important part of me?

So why haven't I been?

Something was shaking at the corners of Peril's brain, shaking and tugging and pulling and trying to come loose, but she couldn't sink her teeth into it . . . she couldn't *remember . . .*

"All right," Ruby said to Queen Scarlet. "You win. If you promise me that Cliff will be safe — I'll give up my kingdom."

"No!" exploded one of Ruby's soldiers, stumbling forward. To Peril's surprise, he was not a SkyWing — he was a MudWing, skinny and tired-looking and spattered with dirt.

"Peril," he said, holding out his talons beseechingly. "What are you doing? You don't want this. Nobody wants this. What would Clay think?"

Peril tilted her head at him. The thing in her mind was really flapping now, but it still didn't have a shape or anything useful that she could pin down.

"Clay?" she echoed. "Who's that?"

CHAPTER 15

In the silence that fell, the only sound was Ruby inhaling sharply.

"It's a spell," she said. "What did you do to her?" She whirled toward Scarlet.

Behind her, in the huddle of SkyWing guards who were now flapping and whispering among themselves, Peril saw two of them slip out into the sky and wheel around to fly south. If they were up to something, she couldn't imagine what it might be, so she decided she didn't need to point them out to the queen, who was in any case quite busy giving Ruby an exaggeratedly shocked expression.

"I didn't do anything at all!" Scarlet protested, batting her wings airily. "Peril is my most loyal subject, just as she always has been. That's why she's my champion and you are going to be dead soon."

"Peril would never just *forget* about Clay," said Ruby.

"How did you erase him from her brain? What kind of horrible animus-touched object did you get your claws on?"

"Hey, I'm not under a spell," Peril interjected. "I just don't know who you're talking about. I don't have a great memory. No need to get all smoky and bothered."

On the other side of Queen Scarlet, orange scales moved, and Peril remembered that her father was there, listening.

Her father . . .

"Clay is the dragon who changed you," Ruby said. "At least according to you. He's one of the dragonets from the prophecy who ended the war. Remember? You met in the arena. You saved his life in the Kingdom of Sand when a dragonbite viper bit him. He's —" She stopped and looked down at her talons. "He's the only dragon who was willing to give you a second chance."

"Well, there's me," Scarlet said smoothly. "The dragon who gave you your first chance and never required a second. That's all you really need to remember. I am the one who cares about you."

That sounded true.

And *not* true.

"Wait. There's Turtle!" Peril blurted. That was the one dragon she could think of who'd ever been friendly to her. He laughed at her jokes, even the ones that Peril hadn't done on purpose. She remembered *that*.

And hang on, why would Turtle be friends with her if she was really Scarlet's dangerous weapon?

He liked me with *my firescales. But without my queen.*

"Who's Turtle?" her father said tensely. He glanced up at Queen Scarlet. "You never mentioned anyone named Turtle."

"ANYWAY," Scarlet said. "We were in the middle of a wonderfully peaceful transfer of power. Ruby, dear, since obviously I can't trust you anymore, I'm going to have to lock you up until I figure out what to do with you. I'm picturing some kind of grand ceremonial execution, maybe to celebrate turning my arena back into an arena, the way it's supposed to be."

"But Cliff —" Ruby started.

"He'll be fine," Scarlet said. "Safe with his loving grandmother. For now. At least until this whole misunderstanding is quite cleared up and the balance of power is right back where it should be. Guards," she added commandingly, "take Ruby to the prison in the Great Hall — the one where we kept Kestrel. Lock her in, and then notify all the cowards in this palace that it's time to come out and swear their allegiance to me."

There was a long, dreadful pause that felt like someone taking a dragon wing and stretching . . . stretching . . . stretching it just . . . beyond . . . its extension . . .

Scarlet hissed dangerously. "Or," she said, "we can all

watch this little prince burn to death, followed by every disobedient dragon in this room."

"Do as she says." Ruby turned to the soldiers behind her. "Whatever it takes to keep Cliff safe. You two — I want you to be the ones to lock me up."

"But, Your Majesty —" one of them began, then stopped as Ruby shook her head.

"It's done," she said. "Let's go. Cliff, I love you, little one. Don't be scared. You're still going to change the world, all right?"

The dragonet nodded, his wings drooping forlornly. He looked back at Peril. "Can I give Mommy a hug?" he whispered. "I think she need a hug."

Peril shook her head. "Sorry, little friend."

Cliff watched Ruby walk out of the throne room, her head held high, and he did a little shake with his wings as if trying to imitate her stance.

"Clear out!" Scarlet snarled at the other soldiers. "I don't want to look at you anymore."

Someone muttered, "The feeling is mutual," as most of the SkyWings filed out. The one MudWing gave Peril an anguished look as he followed them.

"Try to remember Clay," he whispered. "Please."

Soon they were gone, and Peril was left alone with her father, Queen Scarlet, and the little prince.

"Who is Clay?" she asked the queen. "Should I remember him? Do you?"

Scarlet shrugged. "Barely. He's some nobody who thinks he's a hero. Don't worry about it."

"They seemed really sure that I knew him," Peril said slowly. "Ruby said I saved his life — but I don't remember ever saving *anyone's* life. I would definitely remember that, wouldn't I?"

"Maybe she's got you confused with some other dragon," Scarlet said. "This conversation is ever so boring. I'm going to tour the palace to see what other damage my dreadful daughter has done. Vermilion!"

The red dragon poked his head in the door immediately, as if he'd been hovering a clawstep away. "Yes?"

"Are my prisoner towers still in place, at least?" Scarlet demanded.

"Er," he said. "Uh . . ."

"I'll take it that's a no," she said. She let out an enormous, aggrieved sigh. "Those took *ages* to build and they were *genius*. I'm going to have to kill at least seven disloyal traitors to cheer myself up. Fine — you two," she barked at Peril and Chameleon. "Take this dragonet to the tallest spire of my palace and stick him on the highest ledge you can find. Wait. Lizard, can you fly yet?"

"My name isn't Lizard, is *Cliff*," said the prince boldly. "And . . . not so much? I practice lots! But I falled lots, too."

"Good," said the queen. "As long as he can't fly away, he'll be stuck up there. Keep an eye on him until I get back."

She swept out of the throne room with Vermilion, leaving Peril with the bewildering impression that the queen had just run away from an awkward conversation.

Chameleon picked up Prince Cliff and perched him on his back. "Hold on tight," he said. The prince obligingly threw his arms and wings around Chameleon's neck and buried his face.

They flew out the open wall and soared in a circle for a moment, assessing the palace. Peril realized that the tallest spire she could see was the chimney for the crematorium — a long, long tower that carried the smoke of burning bodies as high and far away from the rest of the palace as possible. But sitting on top of it would put them right in the middle of the smoke and the smells, and Peril had a feeling that might be a little traumatizing for Cliff, plus not much fun for her and Chameleon either.

So instead she chose the second-tallest spire, a lookout for guards near the outer wall of the palace. At the top of the tower was a small pavilion with room for five or six dragons to fit comfortably. A shallow hole in the floor was intended as a fire pit, for heating the tower when it was cold or for cooking prey. The walls were open on all sides, but the position of the tower was clearly directed west, to watch for attacks from IceWings or SandWings.

Cliff slid off Chameleon's back and began to prowl around the pavilion. "There's no things to play with here," he complained.

"Use your imagination," Chameleon said unsympathetically.

The prince snorted, flicked his tail at the fire pit, and curled up in a small ball with his wings flopped out to either side. If his intention was to make a point by sulking, it didn't last long, because he was asleep a few minutes later.

Peril sat at the edge of the tower and looked down at the Sky Palace. It still seemed very . . . quiet. Usually there were dragons flying from tower to tower, or coming in with reports, or sailing out with messages. Usually the palace fluttered with activity and wingbeats filled the air.

But not today. Today an eerie stillness suffused the clouds. The mountain peaks looked frozen in time.

Where was everyone?

A light rain began to fall. Peril glanced up and saw darker storm clouds rolling in, thickening the fog around the palace spires. The daylight had a smoky green tinge to it, as if the sky, too, knew that something was wrong . . . something was unbalanced in the world below.

Even the sky rejects the old queen, she thought. *The sky itself chooses Ruby.*

She shook out her wings, trying to dislodge the unfaithful thought.

"How are you feeling, daughter?" Chameleon asked. Peril glanced at him, wondering whether she should call him Soar while he was a SkyWing, or if it was all right to keep just one name in her head for him. He was fiddling with the sheath on his chest as though he were trying to avoid her eyes.

"Great," Peril said. She stretched her wings — her safe, touchable wings — and thought for a moment. Was she still feeling great? She'd been so happy yesterday. But the pretending, and the hatred from Ruby, and Cliff's drooping wings, and this weird feeling of holes in her brain — it was all kind of making her happiness flicker and dim. "A little worried," she admitted.

"Don't listen to those other dragons," said Chameleon. "You're essentially the second in command of this palace. I wish I'd had that much power in my tribe. I'd have made everybody regret every moment of disrespect, every mocking laugh and disgusted whisper."

"Why were they mocking you?" Peril asked. "I thought RainWings were all mellow and calm and friendly and sleepy all the time."

"Ha," Chameleon said bitterly. "As long as you aren't too different, sure. But I had the one problem the tribe couldn't understand: I can't change my scales. You saw my RainWing color. When I'm a RainWing, I'm stuck that way. The same green all the time — no camouflage, no flamboyant emotional outbursts, no self-absorbed displays of clever special effects. I could never play their little RainWing games."

"Oh," Peril said. "Weren't there any other RainWings like you?"

"Not in living memory," he said. "The healers guessed that it was because of my sleep problem — as myself, I can never sleep for longer than a few minutes at a time, an hour at most. They thought it affected my scale-shifting abilities. But knowing that didn't help. Everyone still teased me . . . and then whispered about me . . . and then avoided me. Finally the queen banished me, saying I was making everyone uncomfortable, and perhaps there was a better tribe for me outside the rainforest somewhere."

"Ouch," Peril said. "That seems . . . really unfair, to throw you out for something you couldn't control."

"Exactly," he said. He brooded for a moment, staring down at the fog with hooded eyes. Then he let out a bark of laughter that made Prince Cliff shiver in his sleep. "The joke's on them, though, isn't it? What I can do now — my shape-shifting power — it's far more magnificent camouflage than anything a mere RainWing could accomplish." He held out his orange talons to admire, humming softly with pride.

Peril studied him out of the corner of her eye, wishing she could think of a clever sideways way to find out what she wanted to know. But that wasn't her — clever or sideways.

"How does it work?" she finally asked. Flying at the question directly was the only way she could think of to attack it. "How did you get your shape-shifting power?"

He flicked his tail and looked at her thoughtfully. Peril tried to arrange her face to look deeply, immensely trustworthy.

"Not even Scarlet knows this," he whispered. He glanced back at the prince, who was fast asleep.

A quiver of excitement ran through Peril. A secret! She never got to be the only dragon who knew a secret! *Oh, I forgot to tell Queen Scarlet about the SeaWings having an animus! OK, later, I'll have to remember next time I see her.*

"You can tell me," she whispered back. "There's no one I would tell anyway."

"Not even Queen Scarlet?" he asked.

She shook her head. "You're my father," she said. "You changed my scales and made me safe and normal. My loyalty is to you first, her second."

"Hmmm," he said. "Very interesting. You have a stronger personality than most, um, most dragons I've met."

She wondered what he'd been about to say. Most what? "That is one of the many things most dragons don't like about me," she admitted.

"I like it," he said. "It's something we have in common." He touched the metal sheath around his chest, fiddling with the lock for a moment before it clicked open.

Inside the sheath were two things: a small pouch that seemed to be full of coins or jewelry, and a scroll wrapped in a black leather binding.

Chameleon laid them carefully on the stone between him and Peril, shifting so their backs were to Cliff and spreading his wings so the prince wouldn't see the objects if he woke up.

He tapped the pouch first. "In here are my other shapes. Each piece enchanted with someone new, all my beautiful faces I can take on and off whenever I want to. I have one for each tribe. You've met one of them before, actually."

"I have?" Peril said, her scales prickling.

"Cirrus the IceWing," he said. "Remember him? Queen Scarlet's spy in the Talons of Peace. Perfect because there are so few IceWings in the Talons that they never figured out how little I knew, or that I've never been to the Ice Kingdom. I made him cold and calculating and not much of a talker."

"That's when you first found out about me," Peril realized. "That conversation about Kestrel. You were standing right in front of me."

"Yes," he said. "Scarlet had sent me to find out if the Talons knew where those dragonets went — the ones who stole her prisoner. They didn't, of course. The Talons have always been remarkably useless, in my opinion, apart from gathering the dragonets of the prophecy, and giving Cirrus excuses to practice killing."

He spoke casually, but his words sent a chill down Peril's spine. *He was looking for Moon and Qibli and Winter. Would he have killed them if he found them?*

Would I kill them now, if Queen Scarlet told me to?

She frowned at her claws, hearing that echo in her head again: *I don't kill dragons anymore.*

But why, but why, but why?

"And then I followed you," Chameleon went on without noticing her distraction. He touched the pouch again, fondly. "In my NightWing form. That one's my favorite. I call myself Shapeshifter — isn't that a perfect NightWing name?"

"A bit on the nose," Peril offered.

"Exactly," he said. "Like all NightWing names. I'm quite proud of that shape."

"And then you found me," she said. "But I still don't understand how you make these shapes at all."

Now he touched the scroll, carefully, reverently. "This," he whispered. "It's the strongest magic in the world." He undid the binding and slowly rolled the scroll open. As he did, Peril could see that the first third of the scroll had writing on it, while the rest of the scroll was blank.

"I've never read the whole thing," he said. "I still don't really like reading. I had to find someone to teach me to read so I could understand the scroll in the first place. But then I only had to read the beginning to realize what it could do."

Chameleon rolled it to the end, where it looked like some of the scroll had been torn out.

"And then I had to learn how to write," he added wryly. "*That* was frustrating."

Peril remembered Osprey teaching her how to read and write, although she couldn't hold a scroll or any writing instrument, so it didn't do her very much good. She could read street signs and scrape out messages in the sand, if necessary; that was about it.

Oh! she realized. *That can all be different now! Without firescales — I could read every scroll in the world if I want to!*

That cheered her up quite a lot. She leaned toward the scroll, giving her father her eager attention.

"I write my enchantment here," Chameleon said, brushing the paper with his claw. "I describe the shape I want to shift into, writing the magic into that piece of paper. Then I tear off that part of the scroll and hide it in something — usually an item of jewelry, like a necklace or bracelet."

"Or an ear," Peril said, suddenly remembering a disembodied head changing shape in front of her. *Where was that?*

"Uh — yes," he said. "Only that once, though. I don't use this very often. I've told Queen Scarlet that I have a limited animus power to transform dragons and that it's dangerous for me to do it very much. I don't want her to know about the scroll."

"Why not?" Peril asked. He looked at her in alarm, and she quickly added, "Don't worry, I still won't tell her. But why would you help her as much as you do and not tell her everything?"

"If she knew about this," he said, "she would take it away from me." He started to roll up the scroll again. "And once she didn't need me anymore, she would probably kill me. Besides, I want to be in charge of what this scroll does. It's *mine*. If Scarlet knew I had unlimited power, she'd make me do much more terrible things than anything I've done so far."

He stopped and looked at Peril. "I'm not an evil dragon, Peril. I like the security of having a queen who will pay me handsomely for my services, and I love the luxury of so much treasure. But I'm not going to give anyone all this power, especially not Queen Scarlet. I'm much too smart for that."

"Oh," Peril said. Her mind was spinning a little. Was he implying that Peril wasn't that smart? Would she have given Scarlet that scroll without even thinking about it? Wasn't that what loyalty was about? And if he didn't trust Scarlet completely, why help her at all?

"Have you done anything else with the scroll?" she asked. "I mean . . . couldn't you use it to make your own treasure, somehow, instead of waiting for Scarlet to pay you?"

Chameleon opened his mouth, closed it, and blinked at her for a moment.

"I suppose I could," he said slowly. "Scarlet hired me before I'd gotten very far with using the scroll — she caught me transforming and gave me the option of explaining how I did it, or coming to work for her. I chose option B, obviously. And I haven't wanted to do anything risky that she might find out about.

"I have a very nice life, though," he said quickly. "And so can you, once this kingdom is all sorted out. We'll be her right-claw dragons, and we'll be together. Maybe you can help me come up with clever uses for the scroll. It'll be nice to have family at last."

"Yes," Peril agreed. Family — that sounded amazing actually. She'd barely had a chance to meet Kestrel before her mother died. And if there were any other dragons related to her in the Sky Palace, they'd never introduced themselves.

But something new was starting to bother her. "Wait," she said. "If you're the one who's been helping Queen Scarlet all along . . . does that mean you're the one who put Kinkajou in the hospital?"

Chameleon stared at her for a long moment, the muscles in his jaw tensing and moving like little snakes crawling over one another. He picked up the scroll and the pouch, locking them back in his chest sheath before answering.

"You mean that RainWing who was traveling with the IceWing prince?" he said finally. "She's not dead?"

"You actually were trying to *kill* her?" Peril said, appalled. "Really? She's just a dragonet."

"She's a *RainWing*," he hissed. "She'd laugh at me just as much as any of her tribe, if she'd met me before I found my power."

"Wow," Peril said. She tried to picture the tiny, brightly colored RainWing. "I've never met anyone who hated RainWings before. They're so inoffensive. It's like . . . hating caterpillars."

"I'm not terribly fond of caterpillars either," Chameleon observed. "Nasty crawly things."

Of all dragons, Peril thought, *I should be the one who can understand fury and vengeance and wanting to lash out whenever someone hurts me. He's my father, and she's a drag-onet I don't even know. I should be on his side.*

But still . . . it seemed as brutal and unnecessary as the idea of hurting the little SkyWing prince.

She glanced over her shoulder at Cliff.

Or rather, at the space where Cliff used to be.

She whirled around, her eyes tearing apart the empty pavilion, but there was no mistake.

The SkyWing prince was gone.

CHAPTER 16

"Cliff?" Peril cried. "CLIFF?"

Chameleon flared his wings with a horrified expression. "Where did he go?"

Peril ran to the opposite edge of the tower. Had he rolled off in his sleep? It was a long, long way down. Wouldn't he have woken up and cried out? Wouldn't they have heard him?

She frantically searched the slick wet rocks and rooftops below for a broken red figure.

And then, through a break in the fog, she saw a tiny flapping shape struggling in the rain.

"He *can* fly!" she cried.

"That little liar!" Chameleon yelled. "After him!" He leaped from the tower and plummeted toward the dragonet.

"You know," Peril called, catching up to him, "I thought I remembered that SkyWing dragonets could fly pretty young. That's so funny that Scarlet didn't know that because she avoids dragonets like the plague." Rain pelted her wings and snout and scales, falling harder and harder every moment.

"Shut up and catch him!" Chameleon shouted, nearly drowned out by a crack of thunder. "Or we lose the palace and Scarlet kills us both!"

She wouldn't dare! Peril thought. *Well, all right, she might dare. But she can't, not if I take off this necklace and use my firescales again!*

The locket thumped against her chest, and Peril realized it must have a scrap of that scroll inside of it. Enchanted to make her normal. She hadn't seen her father write it — in fact, it had been all ready for her, so he must have written it before they even met.

Because he loves me. Because he understood what it's like to be different, and he predicted my wish to be normal.

There was something, though . . . something that still felt wrong . . .

Cliff looked over his shoulder and saw the two dragons hurtling toward him. With a terrified squeak, he flung himself through the nearest window and disappeared.

Worse luck, it was a window big enough for a year-old dragonet, but too small for Peril or her father's SkyWing shape.

Chameleon roared in frustration. "You know the palace!" he shouted at Peril. "How do we get in there?" He thumped the stone wall with his tail.

Peril wiped rain from her eyes and looked around. The window was in a covered rampart that led to the central keep of the palace — the keep where the throne room, the Great Hall, and Ruby's prison were.

"Come on," she said, beating her wings. One option was going through the open wall of the throne room, but if Queen Scarlet was in there, things would get ugly fast. A better choice was to fly to the top of the keep and enter through the open roof, like she had done once to rescue Kestrel . . . she shook her head hard. *Who did I do that with? Why is it all fuzzy?*

As they soared up the cliffside, Peril had a dizzying sense of déjà vu — a feeling of wild freedom, terror, and hope that didn't match the current situation at all. She glanced behind her and realized she was expecting to see someone other than her father.

Who?

A moment later they reached the top and dove through the hole into the Great Hall, which was as eerie and deserted as the rest of the palace. Peril saw one or two snouts poke out curiously at the sound of her wingbeats and then vanish in a hurry. A guard stood listlessly by the throne room, but she didn't even look up as Peril flew by.

Down at the bottom of the hall, Ruby was trapped below a grate of metal bars, in the lowliest prison Scarlet had been able to come up with, for her least favorite prisoners. *I guess someone fixed the grate,* Peril thought, remembering her own claws burning through those very bars.

Two SkyWings stood beside the grate, looking less like guards and more like guardians. They were staring up at the commotion of Peril and Chameleon diving toward them, and so they didn't see the small red shape that darted into the room from a hall behind them.

Prince Cliff reached the prison bars before Peril did. He threw himself on top of the grate and reached through, clasping one of his mother's talons in both of his.

"Cliff!" Ruby cried. "Get back!"

And suddenly, a moment before Peril touched down on the stone floor, Ruby came surging out of her cell, flinging aside the crisscrossed bars as if they were nothing.

As if it wasn't actually locked.

Or never really fixed at all.

That's it, Peril thought. *Ruby wouldn't have wanted a prison like that anyway. And the SkyWings who locked her in were loyal to her — they only pretended to do it, enough to make Scarlet believe it.*

She isn't giving up. She's not the mouse her mother thinks she is.

What else is Scarlet wrong about?

The two guards threw their wings open, facing Peril in battle positions, as Ruby cleared the cell in one leap and caught her son up in her arms.

"I *knew* you could do it," she said to him. "You clever, clever, clever little moonbeam."

"I'm not a moonbeam!" he protested, snuggling into her chest. "Today I'm a super-secret stealth agent flier hero of the world."

"Yes, you are," she said.

A deafening roar suddenly shook the entire hall. Peril pressed her talons over her ears, unconsciously trying to make herself as small as possible. This was a familiar roar; a roar that always heralded shouting, scorn, and severe punishments. Queen Scarlet could never hit her, of course, but she'd found plenty of other ways to make Peril's life miserable.

The SkyWing queen seemed to arrive from everywhere at once, her flapping orange wings filling Peril's whole field of vision.

"NO!" Scarlet shrieked, hurtling past the guards and slamming straight into Ruby and Cliff. The three of them tumbled and crashed into the back wall, and before Ruby could stand up again, Scarlet grabbed her neck and pinned her against the stone. Cliff scrambled under his mother's wing and she tightened it around him, glaring at Scarlet.

"You think you're so smart, pathetic daughter," Scarlet hissed. "But your love for this dragonet is a weakness. After I kill you, do you want to know what I'm going to do to him? I'm going to make him fear me. I'm going to make him so loyal to me that he'll forget your name. He'll obey my every command."

"Will not," Cliff said defiantly.

Scarlet ignored him. "I'll use him until he becomes a dragon you wouldn't recognize. By the time I'm done with him, he'd kill you with his own talons if I tell him to."

"Will *not*," Cliff said again, sounding both outraged and scared. "Would *never!*"

"He'll be my adorable little weapon," said Scarlet, "and he'll forget all about you. I will be his everything."

I'm the only one who cares about you.

No one will ever love you except me.

You'll always be a monster to everyone else.

Scarlet's words rang louder and louder in Peril's head. What she was describing — *that's what she did to* me.

She made me obedient. She made me loyal to her. She made me think I had no choice.

But I do.

"Stop!" Peril shouted. She stepped forward, and for a moment the guards wavered, as if wondering whether this was the right moment to sacrifice themselves on her burning scales. She stepped forward again, and they parted before her, leaving her a clear path to the tangle of royal family members.

Queen Scarlet glowered at Peril with narrow yellow eyes. "What did you say?"

"I won't let you hurt Cliff," Peril said. "I won't let you do any of that to him either. It's not right. He's not your toy, and if you can't earn a dragon's loyalty by being a good queen, then you don't deserve it at all." She reached for the black chain around her neck and saw Scarlet's eyes widen.

"No!" Chameleon cried. "Don't take that off!"

Three moons. I am *under a spell.* It hit Peril with the force of a thousand suns. *There's something else in the enchantment. Ruby was right.*

My father betrayed me.

Peril ripped the necklace over her head and dropped it just as the metal began to sizzle.

CHAPTER 17

Everything came rushing back.

Clay Clay Clay Clay, Peril's heart sang. How could she have forgotten about him? How could any spell do that?

She looked around at the circle of watching SkyWings, orange and red heads peering over the balconies and wing-beats bringing in more — Ruby and Cliff trapped under Scarlet's claws — the guards watching her warily . . .

Is this what I become without him? I go right back to being a monster?

She held out her talons. Wisps of smoke were starting to rise from them again.

The firescales aren't what make me dangerous. Even without them, I was as bad as ever, because I was willing to follow her.

Peril lowered her claws and advanced on Scarlet.

"You stay away from me," Scarlet hissed. "Get back. Do

you hear me? I'm your queen, remember? You are my champion. You do what I tell you to do."

"Not anymore," Peril said. She reached toward the scarred ex-queen and Scarlet leaped off Ruby with a shriek. Her orange wings flailed in the air as she backed away from Peril.

"Have you ever wondered what it felt like?" Peril said. "What you made me do to all those dragons? Because it's over now. You are the last dragon I will ever kill."

"Wait," Ruby said suddenly. "Peril, stop."

Stop? Scarlet was so close . . . and Peril finally had the courage to do what she should have done a long time ago . . . and this was the right moment, with everyone watching to cheer her on . . .

But Ruby was her new queen, and if Peril wanted to prove she could be trusted — if she could *ever* be trusted again — she should start by listening to her.

She stopped, keeping her wings spread so Scarlet couldn't escape. "Yes, Your Majesty?" she said to Ruby.

There was a stunned little pause, dappled with growls and hisses from Scarlet, and then Ruby collected herself.

"Don't kill her," Ruby said. "You shouldn't have to. This is my fight." She gently moved Cliff behind her, tucking him back against the wall, and then stood up tall. "Queen Scarlet of the SkyWings, I hereby challenge you to a duel for throne and kingdom."

A gasp scattered around the hall like leaves in a windstorm.

"You don't have to do that," said one of the nearby guards, very bravely, Peril thought. It meant he'd be the first one in flames if Scarlet ended up winning. "*You* are the queen we want, Queen Ruby. Just order us to kill her for you."

"Or me," Peril offered. "Order me to do it."

Ruby shook her head. "I want to take my throne the right way, the way I should have done before if I hadn't been such a coward. I'm going to follow SkyWing tradition, and when I win, no one will be able to question my position anymore."

Scarlet chuckled, smoke billowing from her snout. "When you win? How thrillingly hilarious. After all the challengers I've killed, you think *you* stand any chance at all? My mousy daughter who can barely speak in a room with more than two other dragons in it."

"Let's find out," Ruby said, flexing her claws. "Maybe I'm not who you think I am."

Queen Scarlet started to laugh. She laughed and laughed so much that Peril was extremely tempted to set her on fire just to shut her up.

"Very well," she cried finally. "I accept your challenge. Come at me, daughter."

Peril stepped aside so the two dragons could face each other. Ruby met Peril's eyes, and something entirely new passed between them.

"I'll protect Cliff," Peril said to her. "No matter what happens."

"Thank you," said Ruby. That was all she needed to say. That was more, Peril suspected, than Scarlet had ever said to either of them.

"To the arena, then," Scarlet growled.

Ruby shook her head. "It's full of wounded soldiers and healing supplies. Choose somewhere else."

Scarlet looked momentarily unsettled, but recovered quickly. She glanced around at the gathering crowd, and Peril wondered if she'd choose to fight right here in the Great Hall. *And then maybe Ruby could* accidentally *throw her right into me and I could* accidentally *catch her and WHOOSH no more Scarlet . . .*

Perhaps the same thought occurred to Scarlet, because she nodded at the open roof and said, "Up there."

The two SkyWing queens took off first, soaring toward the sky, and then what seemed to be the entire palace lifted off to follow them, dragons jostling for airspace as they competed for a ringside seat at the fight.

Peril couldn't fly through a crowd like that, not without

seriously hurting someone. She backed up against the wall next to Cliff.

"Hello," he said. "I think today I'm-a be a warrior champion and go swish! swish! with my claws and ROARGH with my mouth and save Mommy."

"Maybe we should stay down here," Peril said. She didn't want poor little Cliff to have to watch his mother die, if everything went wrong and Ruby lost. It probably wouldn't be the greatest feeling to watch his mother kill his grandmother either, even though he had experienced Scarlet's evil firsthand.

"NOOOOOOOOOOOOOOO!" Cliff shrieked at her, making her jump. "I want to SEE IT!"

"Three moons, calm down," Peril said. "I just don't want you to get upset and fights can be very, um . . . upsetting."

"I WON'T get upset!" Cliff shouted. "I want! to SEE! MOMMY KILL GRANDMA!"

Peril had to stifle a giggle. "All right, you bloodthirsty little barbarian," she said. "Let's wait until there's space and up we'll go."

He gave her a sideways look. "You different now?"

"Yes," Peril said. "I'm better now."

"Not a bad guy?" he said.

"Well . . . I hope I'm not a bad guy," Peril said. "I was under a spell before."

"Hmmm," said Cliff. "A spell?" He scampered over and picked up the necklace. "From this?"

"Right," Peril said. She took the necklace and clasped it between her claws, letting it melt into a blackened hunk of metal. "I wasn't thinking for myself. I was thinking what someone else wanted me to think. But I'm all right now." She hesitated. *Now that I'm thinking what Clay wants me to think?*

What if he really was gone from my life? What would I be like then?

Which reminded her . . . she turned to scan the hall, but Chameleon had flown off along with everyone else.

There seemed to be a clear enough path to the roof now. "We can go up," Peril said. "Stay close to me, but don't touch me."

"Why not?" Cliff asked, immediately reaching for her tail.

She flicked it out of his reach. "Because I'm very hot and you'll get burned."

"Oh," he scoffed. "I'm not afraid of me burned."

"*I* am," Peril said. "Be careful — and don't get close to Mommy either. She's very busy right now, so you need to leave her alone."

"Until she WINS!" Cliff sang, vaulting into the air.

If *she wins,* Peril thought as they flew up and out into the driving rain. *What happens to Cliff if she doesn't?*

The roof of the keep let out onto a rocky mountaintop with dizzying views of peaks all around them. Small tufts of fierce little scrub brushes clung to the dirt here and there, but mostly it was all rocks — long overlapping shelves of gray rock and lumps of boulders like giant stone eggs.

Scarlet and Ruby were grappling in the center of a crowd of dragons; some were standing on the rocks and many were hovering in the air so they could watch but also make a quick escape if necessary.

The Sky Kingdom is going to be a mess if Scarlet wins, Peril thought. *She's going to want to kill at least half the dragons here for disloyalty.*

Cliff wobbled over to a boulder that was taller than the others, with a view of the battlefield. The dragons on it saw him and Peril coming and cleared off quickly.

As her talons landed on the slippery wet rock, Peril could see that already the battle was not going well for Ruby. A long slash down her neck and another across her back were bleeding, turning the puddles thick and red around her talons.

The venom-scarred side of Scarlet's face always looked as if it were melting, but the rain slithering off it now made it even worse. The triumphant leer didn't help either; she looked absolutely terrifying and a little bit insane.

Scarlet whirled around and cracked her tail across Ruby's snout. Ruby let out a yelp of pain and jumped back, blinking blood and rain out of her eyes. She tried slashing at Scarlet's nearest wing but missed, stumbling on the slick rocks.

Cliff edged a little closer to Peril's heat. "Mommy?" he whispered.

This poor little dragonet. What do I do if Ruby loses?

Maybe THEN I can kill Scarlet myself. I doubt anyone would try to stop me.

But then there'd be no one left to be queen of the SkyWings, since Scarlet brilliantly disposed of all her heirs.

A jolt ran through her. What about Tourmaline? If Scarlet was telling the truth, Tourmaline was still alive somewhere. And a backup heir would probably be fairly useful right about now.

Where could Tourmaline be? Ruby would know if her sister were in any of the usual SkyWing prisons . . .

But Peril already knew; she could have guessed from the moment she ripped off the necklace. Nobody knew where Tourmaline was, because Tourmaline wasn't herself anymore. Like Peril, she must have been enchanted by Chameleon. She could be anybody now.

Which meant that only Chameleon and Scarlet would be able to identify her.

Peril narrowed her eyes, searching the audience of SkyWings. One thing about Chameleon's disguise as Soar: he blended right in to the rest of the tribe. It took her several minutes to spot him, and then she only did because she caught his eyes watching her instead of the fight.

She pointed at him, and then at the rock beside her. *Come here. Right. Now.*

He wavered for a moment, then flapped down to land, she noticed, in a way that kept Cliff between him and her. *Oh, very brave, Father. Hiding behind a dragonet: classy.*

"I was thinking," he said quickly, before she could speak. "Perhaps we should try a different enchantment. Maybe you don't even want to be a SkyWing anymore. We could both be MudWings! In fact, I could do that right now and we could fly away from here together; what do you think? I hear the Mud Kingdom is . . . tolerable. We could start a new life together. Very far away from whoever wins this fight."

"I don't want a new life," Peril said, bristling. "I want my own life, with all my memories intact, thank you very much."

"You could word the enchantment yourself," he said desperately, or slyly: Peril wasn't sure. She found him hard to read even when he wasn't drowned out by thunder and rain. "We could —"

"No," Peril said. "I'm never letting you change me again. I can't trust you."

He wilted a little, but she was pretty far from feeling sorry for him.

"Now tell me what you did to Tourmaline," she added.

"Me?" he said. "Tourmaline? I don't — I can't even — was there — who's that?"

"Very amusing," she said. "Almost as amusing as your ears on fire would be."

"All right, all right, yes, I changed her," he said. "She was getting too ambitious. Scarlet wanted her out of the way but not dead. She couldn't get rid of *all* her heirs. A kingdom without any heirs is in perpetual danger . . . I think all the queens learned that from what happened to the MudWings a couple of centuries ago. So Tourmaline is still available if Scarlet ever needs her. She just doesn't know it herself."

He trailed off, regarding the battling dragons and rubbing his snout worriedly.

"You shouldn't *do* that," Peril burst out. "You can't just take away a dragon's memory! Turn them into someone completely new! That's horrible!"

"I thought becoming someone completely new was exactly what you wanted," he said, ruffled. "I *like* being different dragons."

"Yes, but you still have your memory when you do that," Peril said. "You know who you are underneath. Tourmaline, I assume, does not."

"True," he said. "But she was safer that way. Otherwise she would have challenged Scarlet and wound up dead before she turned eleven."

Peril shook her head, scattering the cloud of steam that was forming around her as raindrops hit her fiery scales. "You're like eighteen thousand different kinds of untrustworthy. Are you even really my father?"

"Yes," he said firmly. "Kestrel didn't know who I was — she thought I was assigned to partner with her — but I knew her. I am unquestionably your father."

"Wonderful," Peril said. "Such fantastic news. So where is Tourmaline? Is she here now?"

He hesitated, and then nodded.

At the same moment, Ruby let out another cry of pain as Scarlet slammed into her chest, knocking her off her feet. Lightning cracked the sky in half above the fighting dragons, illuminating Scarlet's gloating face as she advanced on her daughter.

"Why isn't Mommy fighting better?" Cliff cried.

Peril looked down at Cliff's anguished face.

"You know what," she said to Chameleon. "Fine. Keep

your secret. It doesn't matter who Tourmaline is, because Ruby has to win this fight." *For the entire SkyWing tribe, but mostly for Cliff.*

"Oh," Chameleon said. "She can't."

Peril stared at him. "Yes she can. Of course she can. What are you talking about?"

"Uh — nothing," he said. "You're right, of course she can."

"Did you do something?" Peril asked. "Did you do something to Ruby like you did to me?"

Below them, Ruby leaped up and sliced one claw across Scarlet's throat, but Scarlet caught her arm and kicked Ruby back into a boulder. Ruby struggled back to her feet, her wings drooping and heavy with rain.

"Well . . ." he said. "Even if I did, it's not working anyway. This shouldn't be able to happen at all. So really, anything could happen next. It's basically like I didn't do anything."

"What did you do?" Peril's wings flared open, scattering warm raindrops all over Cliff. Nightmare possibilities were flashing through her head. He could have done *anything* to Ruby with that scroll. He could have enchanted her to fall asleep whenever Scarlet hit her. He could have enchanted her to go blind whenever she tried to hit Scarlet. He could have enchanted her to lose any challenge battle with Scarlet.

But he'd need a thing to enchant — that's how animus magic works, Peril remembered. *Something with room for a piece of scroll inside.*

She stared wildly down at the battling queens, trying to spot something on Ruby that might be hiding an animus-touched scrap of scroll.

There.

Ruby had one small earring that she always seemed to be wearing — Peril had never seen her without it. A teardrop-shaped pendant hung from it, studded with rubies, and just big enough to open and fit a piece of paper inside.

"Wait here," Peril said to Cliff.

"But —" he protested as she lifted off. "But you said not to interrupt Mommy!"

Peril dove at the wrestling SkyWings just as Scarlet was about to stamp her talons down on Ruby's face. But she must have heard something over the wind and thunder, because she looked up at the last moment, saw Peril hurtling toward them, and leaped backward instead.

Ruby scrambled up and turned to look at Peril, too. "Don't interfere!" she gasped, her heaving sides slick with blood and rain. "I have to win this myself."

Peril skidded to a stop in front of her. "I know — but it's not a fair fight right now. Don't move." She reached out and crushed the dangling earring pendant between two of her claws.

The metal exterior melted first, caving in, and Peril caught a glimpse of something white inside before it crumbled into black ash, and then the whole pendant dropped to the ground.

"Why did you do that?" Ruby cried. "That was a present from my sist — from — I have a —" She stopped, her talons moving slowly to her head as if a glacier were trying to climb out her eye sockets.

Ruby's dark red scales glimmered once, twice, and then faded softly into dark orange instead. Her horns curved inward and her snout lengthened slightly, and her whole body seemed to get thicker and stronger. Not only that, but all her wounds vanished.

"What in the sun . . ." Ruby trailed off, blinking at her newly sharp talons.

Peril was surprised, too. She hadn't expected Ruby to be something different underneath.

"I'm s-sorry," she stammered. "You were under a spell, too. All I know is that it was enchanted to stop you from winning this battle and I — I thought that wasn't fair."

"Tourmaline?" Vermilion said, stepping out of the crowd of gawking SkyWings. "But — aren't you dead?"

"Not yet," said Scarlet. "But she will be soon." She shot a glare at Peril.

"This is Tourmaline?" Peril cried.

"But if I'm Tourmaline," said the transformed queen, "then where . . . or who . . . is Ruby?"

— CHAPTER 18 —

A new flash of greenish lightning illuminated the horrible crooked grin on the old queen's face.

"There is no Ruby," Scarlet said with malicious delight. "I made her up. It turns out when you're the queen, no one questions which dragons you claim as daughters. I invented Ruby completely, exactly the way I wanted her. After all, I've always been disappointed in the daughters I actually had."

If she was hoping for a more devastated reaction, she must have been disappointed. Tourmaline only narrowed her eyes at her mother and lifted her chin, with an expression that looked exactly like one of Queen Ruby's.

"Your Majesty," Peril said to Ruby/Tourmaline. "My advice is to finish killing Scarlet and then figure this out. I have someone who can answer all your questions when you're done."

Tourmaline set her jaw. "Good idea." She launched herself at Scarlet with startling speed, suddenly full of all the ferocity and danger that Peril had expected before. With two quick slashes, she ripped into one of Scarlet's wings, and then sank her claws into Scarlet's shoulders and her teeth into Scarlet's neck.

Another heavy roll of thunder rumbled over their shrieks. Peril backed away from the fight, cautiously working her way to the boulder where Cliff was waiting. Below the thunder and dragon roars, she caught some of the conversations running through the crowd.

"But who *is* that? Where did Ruby go?"

"Did Peril do something to her?"

"Doesn't matter — she's winning now, isn't she?"

"I remember Tourmaline! I thought the queen had her killed a long time ago . . ."

"How does a dragon just . . . change like that? Who did that magic? We don't have any animus dragons in the SkyWing tribe!"

"Wait, I liked Ruby. Can we get Ruby back?"

Peril climbed back up onto the boulder and found dismayed faces on both Chameleon and Cliff.

"I wish you hadn't done that," Chameleon said. "So *publicly*, too. It's going to raise a lot of questions, and I'm afraid it'll be really awkward for me around here if you start pointing talons."

"Oh, I'm sorry," Peril said. "You're right, I should have let Ruby die so you wouldn't have to feel *awkward*."

"Where's Mommy?" Cliff asked, reaching out his little talons. "You said you not a bad guy. You said that! Where did you put her?" He started to cry. "I want *Mommy* back."

Now Peril really did feel sorry. She wished desperately that she could hug him, or at least take one of his talons in hers the way Clay did when he was comforting someone.

"It's all right, little prince," she said, crouching to look him in the eyes. "She has to look like that to win this fight, but she's still your mother. She's just bigger and tougher and a different color, that's all. She still loves you the same."

"Well, she might not," said Chameleon. "That was a whole other personality I built for her, with a lot of false memories in it. She may feel differently about everyone now, even him."

Cliff buried his face in his talons and started to sob.

"STUPENDOUSLY HELPFUL," Peril said to her father. "For our next trick, let's burn out all your teeth one by one."

He took a nervous step away from her. "I only mean that I don't *know* what will happen. Ruby wasn't supposed to be able to challenge her mother at all, and certainly never win. But she's been wearing that personality for over seven years now. Maybe over that much time, it becomes real enough to change like a real dragon would. So she became strong enough to make the challenge. You were strong like that already — I couldn't believe how quickly you overcame the loyalty to Queen Scarlet."

Peril snorted in disgust. "You specifically put loyalty to her in my spell?"

"Of course," he said. "That was my assignment before I ever knew you were my daughter. Remove firescales, add Queen Scarlet loyalty, subtract all memories of Clay."

"I'd say you're the worst dragon I've ever met," Peril said, "but Scarlet still has you beat."

Another wild scream came from the combatants, drawing Peril's attention back to the fight. Scarlet was trying to sink her claws into Tourmaline's eyes, but Tourmaline was holding her off with brute strength, pummeling her underbelly with razor-sharp back talons. Scarlet's scales were more red than orange now, covered in blood from her shredded wing, shoulders, and neck. The rain slammed down on their backs and the clouds seemed to be leaning in closer, as though they wanted to watch the fight as well.

Suddenly Scarlet slipped on the wet rocks and went crashing down on her back; Tourmaline immediately leaped on top of her, digging in her talons.

"You shouldn't have come back, Mother," she said. Tourmaline glanced up at the waiting crowd and shouted, "For the SkyWings!"

And then, with a ferocious *crack*, she snapped Queen Scarlet's neck.

For a long moment, the only sound was the rain falling, pattering on rocks and scales and wings.

Then someone shouted, "Long live Queen Ruby!"

"Queen Ruby!"

"Queen Ruby!" the crowd roared in response.

"I gather that most of these dragons missed the message about who she really is," Chameleon said drily.

"Shows how smart you are," Peril said. "She really is Ruby to them. And if she has all her memories, isn't she really Ruby? What else makes a dragon who she is?"

"Moral fiber?" a voice suggested behind her. "A coherent philosophy of life?"

Peril whirled around. "Turtle!" she cried with delight.

The SeaWing edged out from behind one of the boulders, nervously eyeing the raucous, celebrating SkyWings. He looked extremely wet and somewhat bedraggled. "I, uh . . . came to rescue you?" he said. "Well, to find out what was going on anyway. I heard there was a spell or something? But then I got here and it was very stormy and I couldn't find you and suddenly there were *eight million* SkyWings pouring out of the mountains and a big fight going on and I thought . . . maybe better to stay out of the way until it's over. Right?"

"Yes, smart thinking. If Scarlet had won, it might have gotten a little dangerous around here," Peril said. "But don't worry, I rescued myself. No more spells on me." She gave Chameleon a sharp glance and he nodded frantically. "Plus also I kind of saved the day. It was epic and you missed it."

"Nuh-uh!" Cliff said suddenly, looking up. His face was still streaked with tears, but indignation had broken through his distress. "*Cliff* did that! *I* saved the day!"

"Well, a little bit," Peril admitted. "But it was maybe eighty-five percent me."

"It was NINETY-SIXTY-FIVE-NINETY PERSON ME!" Cliff objected.

"I have little brothers," Turtle said to Peril. "Trust me, you're not going to win this argument."

She couldn't believe Turtle was here! That was something only a friend would do, wasn't it? Come to rescue her from a spell? Deep inside another tribe's kingdom, risking the wrath of a dangerous queen?

"Maybe you do like me after all," she said to Turtle.

"You're a loon," he said. "Of course I do, even when you're scary, which, let's be fair, is most of the time."

"But what if I'm the 'talons of power and fire'?" Peril asked. "Shouldn't you 'beware' me instead of being friends with me?"

"I can beware you and like you at the same time," he joked. "Besides, if I have a choice, I think I'd rather be on the side WITH any talons of power and fire, frankly."

"Cliff! CLIFF!" Tourmaline came bounding over the crowd, barreling through SkyWings with her wings spread. She landed on the boulder and swept Cliff up in her arms. "Did you see that? Mommy won!"

He wriggled anxiously, trying to see her face. "But where *is* Mommy?" he pleaded. "You don't look like Mommy. I want *her*."

Tourmaline winced, set him down gently, and looked over at Peril. Scarlet's blood had almost turned her scales back to red, but the rain spilled over her wings and back, revealing Tourmaline's unfamiliar orange again.

"Do you know how this happened?" she asked Peril. "Do you know who can fix it?"

"Fix it?" Peril asked. She skewered Chameleon with her gaze as he started to sidle off.

"Yes — change me back into Ruby," said the new queen. Behind her back, Chameleon shook his head furiously and clasped his front talons together like he was begging Peril to keep quiet.

Peril blinked away raindrops. "You . . . you want to be Ruby again?"

"I *am* Ruby," Tourmaline answered. "I remember every-thing about being her. All I need is to look like her again."

"But don't you want to be yourself?" Peril asked. "The real true actual Tourmaline?"

Tourmaline put one wing around Cliff and shook her head. "I will be myself. Ruby is the SkyWing queen and Cliff's mother. Now that I know the truth about my sister — about me — I can be even better at both of those things."

If I show her what Chameleon can do . . . I'll be giving another queen his power. He could fly away right now, with no one the wiser about his scroll or his shape-shifting. But if I let him do that, no one will know what he's doing with it. He could end up working for another terrible queen.

I guess it comes down to who I trust more . . . my new queen who always hated me . . . or my father, who betrayed me as soon as he met me.

She thought about Clay, and loyalty, and everything he'd ever said about the family you make and the dragons you should trust and how to make the world safer for everyone.

Peril sprang across the boulder and cornered Chameleon just before he could take off. "This is the dragon you need, Your Majesty."

*   *   *

The queen took them to a quiet library room of the palace, lined with scroll jars, desks, and wooden sculptures of trees that made Peril very nervous, but it was private enough that they wouldn't be interrupted. She kept her wings and tail tucked in close to her and ignored her father when he noticed and gave her a significant "I can still help you with that" look.

"Show the queen," Peril said to him.

"Do I have to?" he asked.

"Yes," said Tourmaline.

"Let's ask my talons," Peril said, lifting them up and nodding thoughtfully at them. "Oh, guess what, they say yes, too."

Cliff giggled. He and Turtle were the only other two allowed in the room, and both watched curiously as Chameleon undid his metal sheath again.

This time he did not reach for his pouch of shapes, and Peril decided not to point that out. She could leave him one secret, since he loved them so much.

But he did bring out the scroll and undid the leather binding with an aggrieved sigh. Carefully, he unrolled the blank end of it along the floor.

"This is what I use," he said. "It's animus-touched."

Tourmaline tilted her head at it. "Where did it come from?"

"I . . . found it," he said evasively. "All I have to do is write an enchantment in here, tear it off, and give it to you to wear, in whatever way you want. Then as long as you wear it, you'll be whatever the enchantment says you are."

Chameleon straightened his shoulders and gave Tourmaline a sly sideways look. "In fact, I could make you anything," he offered. "For the right price, I can make you invincible. I can make you as strong as *ten* dragons. I might even be able to make you a mind reader. Imagine the possibilities! What have you always dreamed of being?"

"Don't trust him," Peril interjected.

"Queen," said Tourmaline. "Both as Tourmaline and as Ruby, that was what I always wanted to become. And I did, without any strange magic." She tapped the scroll. "I want it to say: Turn this dragon back into Ruby, queen of the SkyWings, with all her memories intact."

"That's it?" Chameleon said irritably. "No superpowers?"

"That's it," Tourmaline said. "I want to watch you write it. Do it now."

She leaned over his shoulder, staring narrowly at the page as he dipped his claw in a small inkpot and wrote in scratching, crooked handwriting. As soon as he was finished, he blew on the paper, tore out the written part, and passed it to the queen.

"Check this for me," Tourmaline said, holding it out for Peril and Turtle to examine.

"You saw me write it!" Chameleon protested. "When could I have snuck in any extra instructions?"

Turtle took the paper and studied it on both sides, bringing it close to his eyes. It said exactly what Tourmaline had asked for.

"I think it's the best possible solution," he said, handing it back to Tourmaline. Peril nodded. If this was what the queen really wanted, she wasn't going to argue. She could understand it.

But as for herself, she was staying Peril, exactly the way she was. Firescales and all. No more magic shortcuts to becoming a better dragon, for Clay or for any other reason. In the end, it didn't matter what other dragons thought of her; what mattered was learning to accept the dragon she was and *then* making herself the dragon she wanted to be — the long, hard, real way.

CHAPTER 19

"This doesn't feel like a normal SkyWing party, somehow," Peril said to Queen Ruby.

"That's because it's missing all the fun brutal murder parts," Queen Ruby explained.

They were standing on the top level of the Great Hall, looking down at a mass of dancing, singing SkyWings. Peril watched them hug and spin and clap wings with one another and thought wistfully of the full-moon festival, and how she might never get to dance with anyone in her entire life. Even if she could ever talk Clay into it, she had a feeling he was the kind of dragon with four left talons.

"I mean," Ruby went on, "think about how Scarlet's parties usually went, or what they were for. Actually, you'll sleep better if you don't know," she added to Turtle.

That was true. Peril shivered. Parties for executions, parties for thrillingly bloody arena days, parties for Scarlet's hatching day or Burn's visits that featured all kinds of dragon-killing entertainment. The Sky Kingdom probably hadn't seen a party in twenty years that didn't revolve around Scarlet's gladiator fetish.

But the SkyWings were making up for it now. Somehow about eight orchestras' worth of percussion and stringed instruments had materialized over the course of the day. Now that night had fallen and the storm had passed, music filled the halls of a palace that had once reverberated only with the shrieks of burning dragons.

Peril looked down at her claws. "Your Majesty, I — I'm sorry about the eggs on the brightest night."

"Stop," Ruby said. She drew Cliff closer under her wing; he'd insisted on staying up till midnight, and he looked a lot more awake than Turtle, who kept yawning and leaning on things. "Listen. You were only a dragonet . . . not much older than Cliff . . . and Scarlet was the only parent you ever had. Or friend, or anything. None of the rest of us even tried to see you as a real dragon. I saw a weapon, and that was it. But now . . . I think about what could happen to Cliff if he'd been born with firescales, or if my mother had gotten her claws into him. I think a *lot* about how he'll turn out with me as his mother. So I don't blame you anymore."

"Gosh, *I* do," Peril said. "All the things I — I mean, if you just do the arena numbers, plus the random dragons she disliked, and all the burning, and then you think —"

"Peril," Turtle interrupted. "This might be one of those instances where less detail is the way to go."

"I know it was bad," Ruby said. "But you can make up for what you've done. At least you can try. If we let you try."

"Oh," Peril said. "You bet, of course I'll try. I just need a few more epic battles to the death that I can throw myself into. Point me at some more dragonets in distress! Or viper bites I can tackle! I'm also great at toasting squirrels and boiling water, anytime you need either of those."

Ruby laughed, then glanced at her dragonet and looked serious again. "This should be obvious to everyone who saw you save Cliff," she added, "but just to make it official: you are no longer banished. You are welcome throughout the Sky Kingdom and anywhere Cliff and I go. If you want to move back to the palace, you can."

"Oh," Peril said, oddly embarrassed. "Thanks — I'll think about it."

Is this it? Is this what being a hero feels like? Is this what Clay and Tsunami and Sunny feel like every day?

I thought I'd be more . . . different. I thought suddenly it would be easier to be good — I thought it would come naturally once I did enough good things, or the right big good thing. But I still feel just as muddled about what to do next . . . and I kiiiiiiiiiiiiiind of still want to set that guard over there on fire because I swear he's laughing at me. Not to mention there are lots of wonderfully vengeful things I could do to Chameleon that keep parading through my brain.

Speaking of Chameleon . . . Peril frowned down at a commotion on the level below them.

"Your Majesty," she said. "Isn't that one of the guards who was supposed to be keeping an eye on Cham — er, Soar?"

Queen Ruby didn't have to answer; the guard was now swooping up toward them with a terribly alarmed expression.

"I'm sorry!" she cried, landing next to the queen. "I don't know what happened! I know you said not to let any other dragons in or out, but suddenly there was a NightWing there — a really big one! And he came from *inside* the room and I don't know how he got in there! And he knocked out Harrier with his tail in one blow and then he flew off and the SkyWing was gone! I'm sorry, I'm so so sorry." She flung herself into a deep abject bow.

On the other side of the queen, Turtle sat up, all his sleepiness gone. He looked much more worried and much less . . . puddle-like than usual.

Queen Ruby reached out and raised the guard to standing. "I'm not going to hurt you," she said. "We didn't expect him to run, so it's my own fault for not taking more precautions. Go make sure Harrier is all right."

The guard's face was all relief from snout to horns as she bowed and flew away again.

"How worried should I be?" Queen Ruby asked Peril. "What do you know about that dragon?"

Peril had thought there would be more time — time to tell her queen everything, time to make Chameleon feel safe here and figure out what to do with him and how to deal with the scroll. She hadn't thought he would bolt the first chance he got.

Without saying good-bye. Without thinking about me at all, maybe.

"I know he's really a RainWing," she confessed. "He could use that scroll for anything, but so far he mostly only uses it for shape-shifting . . . I think because he could never change his scales when he was a RainWing. I don't think he would do evil things with it on his own — that was just for Scarlet — but actually, I don't really know him that well."

"He has a NightWing shape?" Turtle said. "And he was working for Scarlet? *Is he the one who hurt Kinkajou?*"

Peril flinched. Why had she let herself forget about that? *Because he offered me everything I thought I wanted.* "Yes," she admitted. "He hates RainWings because they banished him from the rainforest."

"Then we can't let him wander around free with a weapon like that," Turtle said.

"I should have taken it from him right away," Queen Ruby said, shaking her head. "I was trying to reward his cooperation. All right, I'll send out a search party." She saw the anxious expression on Turtle's face and added, "Or six. Six search parties. Don't worry, we'll find him."

She spread her wings and flew down to the throne room with Cliff right behind her.

"We can't wait," Turtle said to Peril. "We have to go after him right now."

"Yes," she said. "But Turtle, one more thing you should know . . . he's my father."

"Wow," he said. "You have had *bad* luck with parents."

"But good luck with friends," she said, grinning at him.

"You big sap," he said. "And I can't even punch you to shut you up."

"You *could*," she said. "That would be pretty funny for *me*."

He flicked his tail at her and lifted off, sailing through the open roof and into the star-speckled sky. Peril followed, feeling the rush of cold wind against her blazing wings. Every moment that she got farther away from that necklace, she felt more and more like herself again. No more troubling or guilty thoughts about Scarlet; nothing but clear memories of Clay.

Can I go back to Jade Mountain now?

Have I done enough?

The questions somehow felt less pressing than they had before. She still missed Clay very much — but she had important things to do. Such as find her father, get that scroll into talons that could be trusted, and maybe help Turtle and his friends stop some big new terrible prophecy, if they'd have her.

"If he's a NightWing, he'll blend right in up here," Turtle called to her, lashing his tail in frustration. One of the moons was almost full, but leftover clouds from the storm hid most of the moonlight from the mountain peaks. "We need help." He angled south abruptly.

"Uh-oh," Peril said. "Tell me we're not off to find a mind reader and an IceWing who might be holding a grudge."

"I left them in that valley," Turtle said, pointing. "They said to signal when I needed them." His scales began flashing, and Peril nearly flew into a cliff, she was so startled. She knew SeaWings had glow-in-the-dark scales, but she'd never seen a dragon use them at night before. Luminescent spirals and shapes like webbed talonprints lit up all along his wings. It was sort of beautiful, in a weird fishy way.

Almost immediately, she saw an answering burst of twin flames from the dark valley below them. Soon after that three shapes rose up to meet them — two of them pale and ghostly, one barely a flicker of shadow.

"You did it?" Qibli said as soon as they were close enough to talk. "You actually . . . rescued her?"

"Not exactly," Peril said.

"But thanks very much for the skeptical tone," Turtle said.

"Is she safe to be around?" Winter asked harshly. "What do you think?" He tilted his head at Moon.

"I AM," Peril said. She thought *MUSHROOMS AND MONGOOSES* at the NightWing as loud as she could, and Moon started giggling.

"That seems like a good sign," said Qibli, giving Moon a smile that reminded Peril of that NightWing who always followed Queen Glory around.

"Guys, we don't have time for a prickly reunion," Turtle interrupted. "Scarlet's ally has escaped and it's worse than we thought. He's a shapeshifter, so he can look like a dragon from any tribe. And he's got this animus-touched scroll that can enchant anything, as far as we can tell."

Moon let out a yelp so loud it echoed off the mountains.

"A scroll?" she cried. "Really? You're sure?"

"Uh — yes," Turtle said. "We saw it."

Moon looked *deeply* agitated now. Peril regarded her with new interest. Was the NightWing hiding something from all of them, even her alleged friends?

"What do you know about this scroll?" Peril asked.

"Nothing!" Moon said. "Was it wrapped in a black leather casing?"

"Yeess," Turtle said, staring at her.

"Maybe you should tell us all the 'nothing' you know about it," Peril suggested.

"I just . . . I heard a story once," Moon said, "about a NightWing scroll from long ago that was animus-touched. It sounds like this could be the same scroll." She fidgeted anxiously, twitching her tail over her talons. "That would be bad. We would really, really need to get it back, if it's the same scroll. That's what I know."

"I was hoping you could try listening for him," Turtle said. "He escaped the palace not long ago, so he can't have gone too far."

"He's in his NightWing form," Peril added. "The one where he calls himself Shapeshifter."

"Very subtle," said Qibli.

"Shh," Moon said, closing her eyes. "I don't think I could pick up anything from way up here."

"Let's fly along the river," Peril said. "I have a feeling he's gone that way. He said something to me about becoming MudWings."

She saw the hesitation in their wingbeats — should we trust this dragon? Are we really going to follow her? But when she turned and swooped away, Turtle was right beside her, and the others weren't far behind.

Going to the MudWings sounded like the next thing her father would do. He wouldn't become Cirrus again, now that Peril knew that shape. She guessed he wouldn't be comfortable underwater, even in a SeaWing form — and he'd have to worry about keeping the scroll dry. Going west to the SandWings meant Queen Thorn, who already had a reputation as someone impossible to corrupt. And she couldn't imagine him returning to the rainforest, either as a RainWing or a NightWing.

But the MudWings were close, and Queen Moorhen had once been Scarlet's ally. She might be willing to take in a strange dragon who offered mysterious power in exchange for treasure.

Peril dove toward the Diamond Spray River, which glimmered like molten silver in the places where moonlight broke through. She remembered Clay swimming away down this river with his friends — heading home to the Mud Kingdom, and away from her. The memory still made her chest ache.

But at least I have that memory.

Suddenly Moon banked right and stopped, hovering in place with her front talons pressed to her head. After a moment, she lifted one of them and pointed.

"I think he's over there," she whispered.

They slipped after her, gliding as quietly as they could.

In a clearing by the river, fiddling with something in his talons, hulked a large black shape.

He made himself enormous, Peril thought. *The kind of scary NightWing everyone has always whispered about.*

Qibli flicked his wing to catch her eye, then pointed to each of them, conveying silent instructions.

A moment later, they landed in a circle around Chameleon. Peril's talons were only an inch from his tail.

"Don't move," she said.

CHAPTER 20

The NightWing reared up, flaring his wings, and he was so big and unfamiliar and angry-looking that Peril had a brief moment of fear that they'd cornered the wrong dragon.

"No, that's him, all right," Moon said. "I'm sure."

Then Peril saw the pouch of shape-shifting jewelry at his feet and the case that held the scroll around his chest. This was definitely him.

"Father!" Peril shouted. "Stop! I don't want to hurt you, but I will!"

"And so will we," Winter hissed, the sound of frostbreath gathering under his words.

Chameleon froze, but Peril still had never seen such a look of fury and disgust on him before.

"That's him," Winter said to Qibli and Turtle. "That's the dragon who attacked us and wounded Kinkajou."

Turtle growled softly in his throat, and Qibli raised his venomous tail, digging his claws into the muddy riverbank.

"But that's impossible," Moon said. "We hit him with my fire and your frostbreath . . . this dragon has no scars, no injuries, nothing."

"It's the enchantment," Qibli guessed. "It probably starts the shape off new and uninjured every time. He just has to take it off, and all the wounds disappear — then when he puts it back on, the scroll makes him a NightWing per the instructions all over again. No lasting damage, ever."

"That's useful," said Peril. She remembered how Ruby's injuries had disappeared when she turned back into Tourmaline. "Is that right?"

Chameleon breathed a small spire of smoke, then nodded. She wished he would say something, instead of just glaring at all of them — at her especially — with those narrow black eyes.

"Listen," she said. "We just want the scroll."

"No," he spat, spikes bristling all along his back.

"Actually, I want the scroll *and* justice," Winter said. "I think he should pay for what he did to Kinkajou."

"Me too," said Turtle.

"Me too," said Moon, "but the scroll is the most important thing."

"And I think taking it from him will be punishment enough," said Peril. Winter snorted disbelievingly and she ignored him. "I'm sorry, Father. But you can't keep it, not after what you've done with it. We can't trust you."

"I won't do anything terrible," he said. "I was only following Scarlet's orders. You know all about that."

"You weren't following her orders when you put Kinkajou in the hospital," Qibli observed. "That was all you."

"And you could have chosen me over her once you knew we were family," Peril said. "You didn't have to betray me by taking away my memories. You could also have stayed and been loyal to Queen Ruby, but it's clear you're not planning on that. You've had choices, and we haven't seen you make any good ones yet."

"But this is an easy one," Moon said. "Give us the scroll, and we let you go."

"Or *don't* give us the scroll," said Qibli, "and get another face full of flames and frostbreath. Wow, try saying that five times fast."

"You'll still have your treasure," Peril said. And she would leave him the scraps of scroll he'd already enchanted with his different shapes. He could still be Soar and Shapeshifter and Cirrus and whoever else when he didn't want to be Chameleon. She knew what it was like to wish for different scales, and she knew how much he needed them, as a RainWing with no scale-shifting powers. "You'll keep having your great life wherever you decide to go. You just won't be able to hurt anyone else."

Winter hissed again.

"But it's mine," Chameleon said, clutching the metal sheath to his chest. "*I* found it, *I* get to keep it. Why should you have it? What makes you all any better than me?"

Peril didn't really know the answer to that question. Was she any better than her father? Did she know these other dragonets well enough to say that they were? What would they do with power like that?

But she knew one thing: she couldn't leave it with Chameleon.

"Give it to us," she said. "Please don't make us fight you for it."

"Or do," said Winter. "I'm ready."

"You think you can hurt me," Chameleon snarled. "But I've made some modifications to this shape since we last met, IceWing. Shapeshifter already had strength beyond any dragon — but now I also have scales that cannot be harmed and flames as hot as my daughter's scales. I foresee a pretty horrible death ahead for most of you."

Peril felt sick. Why hadn't she seen this dangerous, power-hungry side of him before? She didn't want anything bad to happen to Turtle. She was pretty sure she'd even be able to muster some sadness if anything happened to Winter.

"But, Father —" she started.

"What's happening?" Chameleon suddenly shouted. He scrabbled at his chest. "How are you doing that? Stop! It's mine!"

Peril stepped back in astonishment as the sheath unbuckled itself and started to wriggle free of the hulking NightWing's talons. Chameleon held on to it desperately.

"No!" he roared. "You can't take it!"

The metal sheath hesitated, poised in the air as if it were trying to launch itself out of Chameleon's claws. And then it pivoted abruptly and bashed him in the face.

Chameleon yowled with pain, let go of the scroll, and fell back, covering his snout with his talons. Blood was running from one of his eyes.

The sheath bashed him in the face once more, with what looked like the force of a mountain behind it. Chameleon shrieked and Peril guessed that several of the bones in his snout were broken.

"That's enough," she cried. She knew that soon he'd recover from the shock and gather the strength to take off his NightWing shape, and then he'd be healed instantly. But it was still beyond horrible to see him suffering like that. No matter what he'd done, she believed there was a part of him that had wanted to help her . . . that had wanted to be a family.

For a moment, the sheath hovered in the air, as if considering whether to listen to her, and then it spun slowly and floated over to land in Turtle's talons.

"Let's go," he said.

They all spread their wings and lifted off at once; Peril swerved to make sure she stayed clear of the others.

"That scroll is mine!" Chameleon screamed as they flew into the dark clouds. "I'll find you! I'll take it back! You'll be sorry! It's mine, it's mine, *it's mine!*"

Peril glanced left, at Turtle's determined jawline, and then right, at Moon's nervously twitching talons.

Now that they had the most dangerous scroll in Pyrrhia . . . what were they going to do with it?

They flew south for a long time before it felt safe enough to stop; Peril kept imagining she could hear Shapeshifter's ominous wingbeats following them. But soon they came to a part of the mountains that was jagged with canyons and steep ravines, and at the bottom of one of these, they found a cave deep enough to crawl into and set a fire without anyone seeing them from above.

Moon caught some kind of mountain cat for them to eat and they huddled against the stone walls, listening to the rain that had started again outside.

Peril ate her portion in a famished rush, keeping herself on the far side of the fire from the others. Even if Turtle still had his ridiculous healing rock, she imagined it wouldn't go over well if she burned any of them again.

Turtle put the scroll carefully on top of a ledge at the back of the cave. Everyone kept looking at it, although Peril thought that Moon had the most interesting range of expressions about it. What did *that* one mean? And that one? What was she *thinking*?

"You didn't have to do that, Turtle," Moon said finally, breaking the silence. "You shouldn't use your animus power if you can help it . . . maybe you shouldn't use it ever. Aren't you worried about your soul? How do you feel?"

"A little cold," he said with a shrug. "But only the *tiniest* bit evil."

"I'm serious!" she protested as Qibli laughed. "I read about what happened with Albatross."

"My murderous ancestor, I know," Turtle said. "But my enchantments have been so small, and I feel exactly the same as I always have. I think you'll notice if I start turning homicidal."

Moon did not look in the least bit reassured.

"It's all right to use animus magic if you're careful about it," Winter said. "In the Ice Kingdom, our animus dragons used to spend their lives planning one enchantment that would benefit the whole tribe. They used their magic once, for something beautiful and useful, and they were fine all the rest of their lives."

"Huh," Qibli said. "I thought I heard something about an animus IceWing queen who went crazy once, a long, long time ago."

"Oh," Winter said, shifting on his talons. "Maybe. But she — well, she used her magic more than she was supposed to. If it's the queen I'm guessing it was anyway."

"What do we do with this scroll now?" Peril asked. "Should we take it back to Jade Mountain and give it to Clay? And the others?" she added hurriedly.

"Maybe," Turtle said. "But I'm not sure anyone should have this much power, no matter how good we think they are. It can't be good for your soul."

"I think a very wise and good dragon would know how to use it the right way," Qibli objected. "I think we should give it to Queen Thorn."

"Maybe we should give it to Queen Glacier!" Winter snapped.

"We shouldn't give it to anyone," Moon said. "It already belongs to someone."

The fire crackled in the silence that fell, devouring the scraps of wood they had found to burn. Everyone was watching Moon now, and Peril wondered what she could hear in their minds.

"What do you mean?" Winter asked finally, just as Qibli said, "Who?"

"The animus dragon who made it," Moon said. "He put all his power into that scroll so that he could use his magic without damaging his soul. Which is pretty smart, right? He was trying to protect the world from whatever he might become."

"Or give himself unlimited power," Winter observed.

"But doesn't it seem like a good idea?" Moon asked. "If his magic doesn't turn him evil, he'll only do good things with it, right?"

"Doesn't?" Qibli echoed. "Moon. I thought you said this was some ancient legend. So why are you using the present tense?"

"Because —" she started, then hesitated and started again. "Because he's still alive."

"Who?" Winter said, rising to his feet.

"And he's trapped," she said, her words suddenly spilling out like smoke. "I started hearing his voice in my head when I got to Jade Mountain. He's stuck underground somewhere and he's starving and alone and he just wants to get out and this scroll is the one thing that could help him do that. So I said — I said I'd look for it."

"And give it back to him?" Turtle said, then answered himself. "Actually, I guess that's fair. It *is* his magic, after all."

"Moon," Winter growled, his voice low and ominous. "*Who is he?*"

"Well," she said, "first I want you to remember that everything you know about him is two thousand years old and comes from stories told by the dragons who defeated him. You don't really *know* him, even if you think you do."

"DARKSTALKER?!" Winter roared. "ARE YOU SERIOUS?"

"There's no need to yell," Qibli said, standing up as well.

"If the Darkstalker is trapped and starving and alone, that is *exactly* what he deserves," Winter said.

"Oh, really?" Moon countered. "What about the misunderstood NightWing that *you* set free? Wasn't she a legendary enemy of the IceWings, too?"

"Yes, but she didn't have horrible powers," Winter said.

Moon's wings flew open and she rose onto her back legs, growling. "Horrible powers? You mean mind reading and visions of the future? You mean *my* horrible powers?"

"And — uh —" Winter trailed off, glancing at Turtle.

"And my horrible power," Turtle finished.

"Well," Peril said, flexing her talons, "at least he doesn't have mine."

"He killed his own father," Winter said, rallying to his

argument again. "Our IceWing prince. Isn't your whole tribe terrified of him?"

"Yes," Moon admitted. "But they don't know him either."

"And you do?" Qibli asked.

The question hung in the air, and Peril noticed for the first time the intensity in Qibli's eyes as he looked at Moon. She couldn't interpret it exactly, but she got the feeling there were several layers to the question he was asking. Layers like *if he's so important to you, why didn't you tell us about him before?* and one she especially recognized: *do you like him better than me?*

Moon looked away first. "Maybe," she said. "I think so. I don't know."

"I can't let you use this scroll to free the Darkstalker," Winter said.

"What you *can't* do is order me around," Moon said sharply. "What you can do instead is have a rational conversation with me, and listen to me, and try to talk me out of it if you must."

"But not right now," Turtle said. "Right now we should all sleep, and then we can talk about it in the morning. All right?"

"I agree," Qibli said.

"Fine," said Moon.

"Fine," said Winter.

Peril found herself wondering again if friends might be more trouble than they were worth. She was quite glad *she* was not snarled up in this fight.

"I'll sleep outside," she offered, standing up.

"In the rain?" Turtle asked.

"It won't bother me," Peril said. "And I've been told I'm a restless sleeper."

"Oh," Turtle said, eyeing her wings nervously. "In that case, sure, absolutely, you bet, great plan."

Peril shot him a grin as she went out of the cave into the rain. There was a somewhat sheltered spot at the base of the cliff, and she huddled there, thinking about the scroll and the argument and whatever this Darkstalker was, until she finally fell asleep.

And for the first time in years, her dreams were peaceful.

No furious Queen Scarlets chased her through winding hallways with too many doors. Nobody burned between her talons. There was no fire, no smoke, no death or screaming.

Just long, quiet, dreamless slumber.

"Peril? Peril?"

She was awoken by something poking her gently in the shoulder, followed by Turtle yelling "AAAH!" and leaping backward as the stick he'd poked her with burst into flames.

Peril stretched, yawning. "Well, what did you think was going to happen?" she asked. And then she noticed the two serious faces lined up behind Turtle.

"Uh-oh," she said.

"Moon's gone," said Turtle. "And she's taken the scroll with her."

CHAPTER 21

The world after the storm was dazzling; sunbeams glinted off all the new puddles and the sky felt as though it had just taken a dive in a lake. It seemed as if more dragons were out flying than Peril had seen in ages — everyone wanted to spread their wings in the beautiful air. She saw a lot of SkyWings especially and realized guiltily that they should have let Queen Ruby know the scroll was safe.

Except apparently it wasn't very safe, after all.

"She wouldn't," Winter fretted as they flew south. "She *wouldn't.*"

Qibli was silent for once, deep in thought.

"Uh," Turtle said, "maybe she —"

"I thought we were all going to talk about it!" Winter yelled.

"Maybe she didn't think you'd be a good listener," Peril suggested. "I mean, I haven't known you very long, and even I can already see that."

"I *listen*," Winter growled, "when there is something *worth hearing*."

"Yeah, I don't think that's the same thing," Peril said, shaking her head.

"You can fly faster than us," Qibli said suddenly. He twisted himself in the air so he could look at Peril. "You can fly faster than *her*. Maybe you can catch her."

"Oh, yes," Peril said. "Probably. You guys are slowpokes. It's like flying with a trio of banana slugs."

"So go!" Turtle said wildly. "Fly as fast as you can! Stop her before she sets him free!"

"Um . . . all right," Peril said. "Except . . . how do I do that?"

"Just tell her what a bad idea it is!" Winter said.

"Ah, OK," Peril said. "So, stop her with . . . words."

"Well, right, don't set her on fire," Turtle said. "Let's be clear about that."

"Are you sure?" Peril said. "It would be very efficient. I bet it would stop her right away. Just a tiny bit of her tail — I'm kidding, I'm kidding!"

She hadn't *exactly* been kidding, but she could tell from the expressions on their faces that she'd better act as though she was.

Not that she *wanted* to use her firescales on Moon, but if

the alternative was some big ancient nightmare dragon rising from the earth, then shouldn't all the options be open?

Qibli looked close to panicked, though, and Winter was giving her the MOST suspicious, untrusting face, and even Turtle looked worried about this plan, so: No. The answer was evidently "let the nightmare dragon escape rather than harming even one of Moon's scales."

"If she insists on doing it, tell her at least to wait for us," Qibli pleaded. "Tell her she shouldn't release him alone."

"All right," Peril said, flicking her wings to rise to a higher updraft. "I'll try." *But I suspect I might be exactly the wrong dragon for this particular mission.*

"She'll be close to Jade Mountain somewhere!" Qibli called after her. "He must be buried near there if that's where she could hear him!"

"Got it!" Peril called back.

She was surprised when she hadn't caught up with Moon by midday. Either the NightWing had a much bigger head start than Peril had guessed, or she flew a lot faster than Peril would have expected.

Peril stopped only once, to drink from a mountain lake, and spent the rest of the day flying as fast as she could. She was exhausted when the first stars of the evening began to emerge and she saw Jade Mountain starting to fill the sky ahead of her.

Clay's in there, she thought with a thrill of excitement. *I could see him tonight. I can tell him everything that's happened.*

But first she had to stop Moon.

Peril slowed down as she got closer to Jade Mountain. She began to scan the peaks around her with her eagle-sharp eyes, looking for unusual movements.

Once she swooped down only to discover an extremely startled moose; the second time, she nearly got a snoutful of porcupine quills.

But on her third try, she found the dragon she was looking for.

Moon wasn't exactly hiding. She was sitting on a grassy slope on the western side of a mountain not far from Jade Mountain. The sunset cast golden rays over her huddled form and her shadow sloped like a long second tail up the hill behind her.

Peril looped around overhead, studying the ground around Moon until she spotted a boulder where she could safely land. It wobbled slightly as she thumped down, threatening to tumble into the narrow ravine nearby, but she steadied it with her claws.

The NightWing didn't look up. She was curled over the scroll, reading it so intently that her claws were crushing the binding where she held it.

"Um," Peril said. "So. Hello. I've been instructed not to set you on fire. In case you were worried," she added hastily.

Moon raised her head and Peril realized that her eyes were full of tears. In fact, her whole face was full of tears; she looked as if she'd been crying for a while.

"Yikes," Peril said. "I'd offer you a hug, but . . ."

"I just wanted to hear him again," Moon said. "I wanted to tell him we found it — to talk to him and remember why I trusted him. But then I started reading, and he clearly didn't want me to, and I found this." She trailed off, touching the scroll with one mournful claw.

Peril tilted her head at the paper. She could see that Moon was on the page where the writing stopped and the rest of the scroll was blank. But she couldn't read the letters from where she was, and she didn't dare get any closer.

"What does it say?" Peril asked. When Moon stared into space instead of answering, she added, "Hey, *I'm* not a mind reader. Different horrible power over here, remember?"

"Stop talking!" Moon said sharply, making Peril jump. "Oh, not you," she said to Peril. "Him."

"He's talking to you right now?" Peril said. "That's . . . creepy."

"He has trouble reading your mind, too," Moon said. "Although he agrees it's a lot less infernoesque than it was before you went to the Sky Palace."

". . . Yay?"

"A dragon's not a *thing*!" Moon suddenly exploded, talking to the air again. "You shouldn't be able to enchant someone like that! It's *wrong*. Don't you — no, stop, it doesn't matter how bad he was. *This*." She jabbed the scroll so hard it ripped a little. "*This* is the cruelest thing I've ever read."

"OK, you really have to tell me now." Peril was itching with curiosity.

"I am," Moon said. "I am going to tell her. When you do something this terrible, you kind of cancel out any privacy rights." She turned to Peril. "Remember how Winter said that Darkstalker killed his father, Prince Arctic?"

"Yeah," Peril said. "That confused me a bit. Why was his dad an IceWing?"

"Long story, not important," Moon said. "I mean, except to the IceWings. Anyway, the other rumor I'd heard about Darkstalker was that he did something so awful that it terrified the entire NightWing tribe into abandoning their city and going into hiding, so that he would never find them again if he ever came back. They thought he was gone, maybe dead, but they still uprooted the entire tribe to hide from him, just in case."

"Yeesh. And I thought my tribe hated me," Peril tried to joke. She was starting to get a creepy-crawly feeling under her scales. This menacing dragon was buried alive some-where right below their talons?

"Well," Moon said, "now I know what it was. Yes, I do. I'm sure. If I saw a dragon do this, I'd go into hiding, too."

"YES?" Peril said impatiently.

Moon dropped her voice. "He used his magic *on his father.* He enchanted him, as if Prince Arctic was no more than a necklace or a rock or a piece of cheese."

"Oooh," Peril said, momentarily distracted by the idea of an enchanted piece of cheese.

"The spell is right here," Moon said. She spread her front talons on the scroll, starting to cry again. " *'Enchant Arctic the IceWing to obey my every command.'* That's it. It's that simple. What did you make him do?" she demanded. "You made him kill himself, didn't you?"

"Whoa," Peril said. "Is that possible? That could happen? Could Turtle do that?"

Moon gave a furious shake of her head. There was a long pause, and then she yelped, "Disembowel? Did you seriously just say disembowel?"

"Who disemboweled who?" Peril asked. "Oh, GROSS, did Arctic disembowel himself? That is much worse than any-thing that happened in the arena. Oh my goodness, Scarlet would have loved to get a self-disemboweling dragon in her arena. She's dead, by the way, did we mention that?"

But Moon was lying down on top of the scroll now, pressing her talons over her ears with her eyes closed.

Peril wondered if she should try to get Moon away from Darkstalker's voice, but she couldn't think of a way to do that without either touching her or throwing rocks at her to get her attention, which seemed a little heartless considering what Moon was going through.

So she decided to watch over her and wait for the others. That seemed like a sensible plan of action.

She glanced around, found a tree that was growing at an angle out of a ravine, and lit its branches on fire. That should help Turtle, Qibli, and Winter find them.

It felt like hours of Moon not moving and Peril sitting there watching her not move. But at last Peril heard wingbeats, and she turned to see the other three dragons straggling up, looking much the worse for wear after flying all day. Turtle in particular looked like the world's unhappiest squashed frog.

"There she is!" He gasped.

"Moon!" Qibli and Winter cried at the same time.

"And hello to you, too," Peril said.

The two of them landed and ran over to Moon, but Turtle came over to Peril's boulder first.

"What happened?" he asked. "Has she —?"

"No, she hasn't freed him," Peril said. "I don't think

she's going to. She's had some bad news, though, so don't be a phlegm-snorting ratbreath at her!" she yelled over to Winter.

Qibli crouched beside Moon, covering her gently with one of his wings. "Tell us what happened," he said. "Is he talking to you right now?"

"Yes, and he won't shut up," she said, sitting up and wiping away her tears. "Winter, you were right. We can't free him." She passed the scroll to Winter, who let out an almost imperceptible sigh of relief. Qibli breathed out a small flame so they could both read it.

"Whoa," Qibli said after a moment.

"We absolutely can't free him if he can control other dragons that way, that *easily*," Moon said. "And we can't free him because he's the kind of dragon who thought of doing it in the first place." She listened for a moment. "He says he promises he won't ever do that again. Darkstalker, how can we trust you? No one could ever stop you, with a power like that. *No*, stop, I don't want to see another fairy-tale vision. I'll have my own visions, thank you very much."

Winter let his wings drift softly down as though they were heavy weights he could finally drop.

"So what do we do with it?" Qibli asked, taking the scroll from Winter's claws. He brushed one talon lightly across the blank space. "I was thinking about it today while we flew.

We could do a lot of good with this. We could use it to protect our queens. I could enchant something so that Thorn will never die, or make her palace immune to attack. Moon, think about it — we could enchant something to make all the NightWings love Glory. You know how many of them hate her, probably better than anyone because you've seen into their minds. But imagine if they all loved her instead? What if she could rule without the threat of assassination hanging over her?"

"She wouldn't want that," Moon said. "She wouldn't want enchanted obedience or fake love."

"How about fireproof scales, at least?" Qibli said.

Ooooo, Peril thought. *We could give all my friends fireproof scales! Which I guess means Turtle. Turtle could be fireproof and safe from me, too!*

Qibli went on, holding the scroll closer. "Or something that could warn Glory before someone tries to kill her? Wouldn't that be a good idea? And then you wouldn't have to use your own powers to help her . . . you could do whatever you want with them."

Moon put her talons to her head. "He really doesn't love this conversation."

"If we're in the business of protecting queens with magic," Winter growled, "we should include Queen Glacier. She's a good queen, too."

"And what about my mom?" Turtle interjected. "Or Queen Ruby, for Peril?"

"But if we enchant all the queens to never die or be magically protected or whatever," Peril said, "then . . . won't we end up stuck with the same queens forever? Wouldn't that be bad, too?"

"Not in the case of Queen Thorn," Qibli said stubbornly. "Look, the three of you have these crazy gifts and you're figuring out how to use them safely, aren't you?"

"Shush!" Moon whispered, closing her eyes. "I've been fine without you!"

Qibli paused with a puzzled expression.

"Not you," Peril explained. "The crazy dragon in her head."

"So if I can trust you with your powers," Qibli said, "couldn't you trust me to take care of this one? To think carefully about the consequences and only use it for good?"

"*You?*" Winter snarled. "By yourself? We just let you saunter off with the most powerful talisman in the world? Why should you get it instead of me? Maybe I should take care of it."

"Or maybe all of us together?" Turtle suggested, but no one was listening anymore.

"You just flew off and abandoned us in Possibility!" Qibli shouted at Winter. "You were really mean to Moon and you haven't even apologized!"

Winter opened and closed his mouth, looking at Moon with an oddly heartbroken expression.

"So how could we trust you?" Qibli demanded.

"At least I'm a *prince* and have some *experience* making decisions to help my tribe!" Winter shouted.

"Oh, awesome logic!" Qibli shouted back. "You're royalty, so you've always had power, so you should get to keep any new power that comes along?"

"Stop fighting!" Moon cried, covering her ears again. "All of you! Darkstalker, stop yelling at me!"

Qibli and Winter were too busy roaring at each other to hear her. Turtle was curled in a ball below Peril's boulder with his wings around him, looking indecisive and worried.

Fighting over power, Peril thought. *Like every dragon ever. But it's not their power, it's Darkstalker's, and they want to use it, the same way Scarlet used mine.*

But that scroll is too dangerous to be in this world. Even if a good dragon controlled it . . . even if it didn't change that good dragon to have that much power . . . even if we could somehow guarantee that it would never fall into evil talons . . . it shouldn't exist.

Look how good dragons are fighting over it already.

Nobody should be the boss of someone else's magic.

And nobody else should ever be hurt by that scroll.

Peril sidled to the edge of the boulder, hopped down onto the grass, hurried through the scorched path she made toward the fighting dragons, and paused right behind Qibli.

The SandWing didn't notice her. He swept his talons wide, shouting something at Winter about being careful.

And Peril reached out and lifted the scroll right out of his claws.

There was a heartbeat of silence as Peril flew back onto the boulder. She sat down and held out her talons, and the other dragons turned around, and they all watched the scroll burn, burn, burn into tiny black ashes.

As the last piece of the scroll flickered out of existence, Peril brushed the ashes off her scales.

"There," she said. "That solves that problem."

Now nothing can set the Darkstalker free, and no one can abuse his power.

She looked down and saw Turtle smiling up at her. Moon's expression was all relief as well, so, despite the shock on Winter and Qibli's faces, Peril felt a sudden, clear bolt of *that was the right thing to do.*

For once she was sure, and not because someone else was telling her what the right thing was, but because she could feel it in her own bones.

I did it. I saved the world. And Clay wasn't even watching.

Even if he never knows about it, I'll *still know I did the right thing.*

She lifted her head to the rising moon, taking a deep, tranquil breath.

Wait. Why was the moon wobbling?

It wasn't the moon. It was the ground. The ground was shaking, harder and harder, an earthquake trembling through all the veins of the mountain. Peril's boulder toppled into the ravine and she had to leap into the air, pounding her wings to get as far away from the shuddering hillside as possible.

The other dragons threw themselves aloft, too.

"What's happening?" Turtle yelled. "Is Jade Mountain falling? Is this the prophecy?"

Peril twisted in the air to look toward the academy. *Clay.*

But Jade Mountain wasn't moving. Only this mountain was, and in fact, it was doing more than shaking and dropping giant rocks everywhere.

It was *splitting apart.*

An enormous crack appeared in the earth, and out of the darkness rose the hugest dragon the world had ever seen. Silver scales glittered in the corners of his eyes and along the underside of his black wings. His bones were visible under his skin; he was long and frighteningly thin, with a narrow handsome face, long twisted horns, and eyes as black as underground caverns.

Darkstalker stretched his wings out to their fullest reach, as wide as the mountain itself. He swiveled his neck, expanding in every direction, like a dragon who hadn't been able to turn or stretch or move in two thousand years.

And then he smiled down at Peril, a smile that was all teeth, somehow menacing and charming at the same time.

"Ah. That's infinitely better," he said. "Nice to finally meet you, Peril. Thank you so much for your help."

EPILOGUE

Starflight was working late in the library — or was it early? He wasn't sure how long he'd been in there, since he no longer needed light to work by. But he thought the sun was not yet up when he heard tiny footsteps coming into the room.

"Hello?" he said. He tried to run through all the students in his head. Small talonsteps, light — but not Kinkajou — with an extra flap sound when they hit the floor. SeaWing talons. "Anemone?" he guessed.

"Yes, it's me," said the little SeaWing princess.

"What are you doing awake?" he asked.

"I had a nightmare," she said, "and then something woke me. Didn't you feel it?"

"Feel what?"

He heard her cross to the wall of windows. It sounded as if she put one talon on the translucent leaves and stood for a moment quietly, without speaking.

"Something that shook the earth," she said at last, so softly that he wondered if he would have been able to hear her before, when he could see.

"I didn't notice anything," he said.

A small sound — Anemone's wings shivering together.

"It felt," she said, "like someone slithering over my grave."

WINGS OF FIRE

will continue . . .

Turtle crouched lower, pressing his underbelly into the ground, and shook his head at them.

"Let's hunt now, as Darkstalker suggests," Qibli said, nudging Moon, "and figure out what to do next after that." He shot a significant glance at Turtle.

Oh no. That glance had a meaning, a message. Qibli was expecting Turtle to do something, and Turtle had a bad feeling that "something" wasn't "Turtle flying all the way back to the Kingdom of the Sea, finding a deep trench, and staying there forever." A queasy, tense feeling started bubbling through Turtle's stomach.

"Good idea," said Winter.

Moon nodded, and then *she* gave Turtle a meaningful look, too.

By all the moons, what did they think he was going to do? Attack Darkstalker, like Peril had? Obviously that wouldn't work. If Peril couldn't hurt him, Turtle certainly wouldn't be able to.

Did they want him to hide them as well? He winced. He should have thought of that sooner. A good friend, a better dragon — a hero — would have thought to protect everyone instead of just hiding himself. *But they all wanted to talk to Darkstalker, didn't they? I just wanted to hide. That's what I always do.*

As the dragons flew away, veering southwest, Qibli twisted in a spiral, looked at Turtle again, and flicked his tail in the direction of Jade Mountain.

Oh, Turtle realized. *They want me to go warn the school. I can probably do that without messing it up.*

I think.

For a moment, Peril hovered mutinously in the sky behind them, and then she swooped down to Turtle.

"Aren't you coming, too?" she asked. "Don't we all have to follow his grand mighty lordship SinisterFace?"

Turtle shook his head and held out the stick. "He can't see me," he whispered. "I hid myself from him."

Peril's face lit up. "Of course!" she said. "That's awesome! You have animus magic! *You* can kill him!"

"Oh," said Turtle, flustered. "No, I — I don't really — kill anyone." A brief flash of scales and blood darted through his mind, and when he looked down, he saw his claws curling dangerously. He jumped and shook them out until they looked like his own talons again. "That's not my thing," he said, tamping down a wave of panic.

"I know, I know, it's my thing," Peril said, "but I *can't* kill him, because of his *stupid* magic, GROWL. So you have to. Don't worry, it's not that hard, and it would be such a relief — for me, I mean — because I'm having this feeling — I don't know what to call it, but it's kind of big and heavy and annoying? And it's filling me all up inside like everything is awful and it's all my fault? Like maybe all the bad things in the world are my fault? I really don't like it, so if you can make it stop, that would be the greatest."

"I think what you're describing is what we call guilt," said Turtle, "but it's not your fault he tricked us. I still think you did the right thing, burning the scroll."

"Well, thanks, but the universe disagrees with you," Peril said, jerking her head at the enormous crack in the side of the mountain.

"Peril!" called one of the dragons in the distance.

"Good luck," Peril whispered. "Make it something really cool, like his insides exploding. Or his face falling off. I'm kidding! I'm a little bit kidding. I mean, insides exploding would be pretty cool, right? Never mind, it's up to you! Destroy him and save the world! Three moons, I wish I could do it!" She took off and flashed away, fast as a firework.

Turtle shivered.

Save the world?

That's not my thing either. I would definitely mess it up. That's way, way too much pressure.

I'm clearly not a hero.

He raised his eyes to the shadowy peaks of Jade Mountain.

But I know where I can find some.